Shattered Image

J.F. MARGOS

Shattered Image

Steeple
Hill®

Published by Steeple Hill Books™

STEEPLE HILL BOOKS

Steeple
Hill®

ISBN 0-373-78520-8

SHATTERED IMAGE

Copyright © 2004 by J.F. Margos

Printed in U.S.A.

This book is dedicated to my father,
Louis Gregory Margos, Jr., who didn't live to see me
complete this work, much less to appreciate its
publication. He was an amateur (only in the sense of
wages) race driver, a master mechanic and a machinist
and heli-arc welder with a penchant for restoring classic
Mustangs. He taught me some of the best things I know,
including an appreciation for great automobiles and the
proper way to take a hairpin turn. He was father, hero,
teacher and friend. I love you, Daddy. "Drive on!"

Louis Gregory Margos, Jr.

1922–1994

May his memory be eternal.

ACKNOWLEDGMENTS

First of all, I would like to thank my mother, who never faltered in her support of me during all my writing projects. She made sacrifices to assure my success, and I could not have accomplished any of this without her. I love you very much, Mom.

Also, thanks to my two sisters, Carol and Jill, who are my best friends, and buck me up when I'm down. Special thanks to Carol for shooting my photo. Thanks to my brother-in-law, Myron, for helping me with all the stuff I don't know how to do, and to my niece and nephew, Jeni and Gregory, for just being themselves. Also thanks goes to my dear friend, Sue Stevens, who constantly gives me moral support, and kicks my rear as necessary. Thanks also to Mary Long (aka the "Kid"), who gives pretty good advice for a youngster. Thanks also to my bud Linda Wilson, who has shared friendship with me for all these years, and has ever been a supporter of my wacky dreams.

Thanks to my godfather, Deacon George Bithos, and his great wife, Presvytera Ria, for all their support and understanding, and for being part of my family and letting me be part of theirs. Σας αγαπω.

I would also like to thank my Spiritual Father, Fr. Jordan G. Brown, who advised me in many spiritual areas, both as background for this book and just in general over the many years we have been friends and spiritual relatives. Σας ευχαριστω, Πατερ. Σας αγαπω.

To my friend, John Esper, for brainstorming on the title. Nice work, dude. Special thanks goes to my agent, Helen Breitwieser, who believed in me at a time when I had begun to lose that belief in myself. I did not expect such steadfast encouragement, advice and undaunted support. I am blessed, Helen, by your professionalism and your friendship.

Thanks also goes to my mentor in business, and attorney, W. Robert Dyer, Jr. Bob, you took a stupid kid and educated her. The things you have taught me have proven invaluable indeed. I don't know where I'd be in life without your guidance and support—I just know I'm glad I won't have to find out.

Finally, it is fitting and right that we should all acknowledge all the women and men who served in the Vietnam War, but in particular those women and men who served so valiantly in the medical field, facing death to save life. I would most especially like to acknowledge and thank my friends Doyle Dunn (who served in Vietnam in the American Red Cross) and his wife, Lauri Dunn, R.N., former captain in the United States Air Force and a Vietnam veteran. Both Lauri and Doyle were an invaluable resource to me in the writing of this book. Thank you so very much for all of your help to me, and for serving our country in such a difficult time.

Thanks and acknowledgment to the great teams at CILHI (Central Identification Laboratory Hawaii), who make incredible sacrifices and go to the far reaches of this planet to bring home our departed soldiers.

I would also like to acknowledge and pay tribute to all of those Americans who died in Vietnam in the service of our country (8 women and over 58,000 men) and to the many—too many—who still remain Missing In Action. As of this writing, there are still more than 1,900 Americans missing in action from the Vietnam War— lest we ever forget.

May their memory be eternal.

"Of old Thou hast created me from nothing.
And honoured me with Thy Divine Image
But when I disobeyed Thy commandment,
Thou hast returned me to the earth whence I was taken,
Lead me back again to Thy Likeness,
Refashioning my ancient beauty."
—Christian funeral chant

❧ *Chapter One* ❧

The dense fog slithered up the riverbank, coiling itself around the traffic light ahead of me and partially
obscuring the green glow until I was underneath it.
With daylight barely peeking over the limestone
cliffs on the other bank, the fog was an especially un-
wanted handicap. I plunged the clutch pedal into
the floor and, feeling the ball of the gearshift lever
in the palm of my hand, I eased the stick down into
second, slid the clutch slowly out of the floor and appreciated the rumble of the downshift and the tug
of the engine braking. With my left palm I wheeled
the car into a left turn and began my descent down
the hill to the low-water bridge below the Tom Miller
Dam. They called that machine of mine a Mustang,
but it had a roar and rumble more like a wildcat.

I pulled the car over to the edge of the road when I reached the island in the middle of the bridge. Red Bud Isle they called it, but on that morning it was a gray silhouette on gray water shrouded in a thick, gray mist. I was sick of this weather and ready for spring and Texas sunshine.

I could see red and blue strobing lights through the underbelly of the fog. Bones found on the riverbank of Red Bud Isle had attracted a large and serious crowd, and I was about to become part of it. It would be my job to put a face back on the deceased.

As I turned off the key, I saw Malcolm walking toward the car. His uniform looked as if he'd slept in it.

"Well, Toni, I could sure hear those wheels comin' before I ever saw them."

"Uh-huh."

"Wow, what a machine. You know Steve McQueen drove one like this in *Bullitt*."

"Mine is a '65."

"It's just like the one McQueen drove."

"McQueen's was a '67. Where's Chris, Malcolm?"

"Sorry, Toni, off to the right-hand side of the bridge here, and then down on this side of the island."

I began to walk toward the area to which Malcolm had directed me.

"Toni, can I drive it sometime?"

"Absolutely not, Malcolm," I called over my shoulder, stifling what I really wanted to say. Somehow Malcolm always brought out the worst in me. I should have been more patient and tolerant. Satan sends the simple to make us stumble.

It was cool out and the dampness of the fog added even more of a chill. I was wearing my jeans and black western boots, with the pointy toes like a real Texan, and an old faded yellow T-shirt. Most people would have worn a light jacket in the cool air, but I was enjoying it in my shirtsleeves.

This was the least favorite part of my job as a forensic sculptor, but a necessary part of it nevertheless. Luckily, most of the bodies I saw in my work were devoid of flesh—a far cry from the sights I had seen in Vietnam as a nurse.

I made my way through the redbuds and other trees that covered the islet. The trees were dense and the underbrush was thick in between them. Boots and jeans were definitely the right gear to be wearing. Straight in front of me, several hundred feet beyond the tip of the island loomed the concrete face of the Tom Miller Dam. The soft rushing of the water from the hydraulic power plant provided backup for the mourning doves cooing their morning song. As I made my way through the foliage, the smell of damp earth, tree buds and tall grasses moistened by dew filled the air. The fog was lifting with the sunrise and thinning to a wispy ribbon overhead and I could see the back of Dr. Christine Nakis, the Travis County medical examiner, near the island's edge.

Her short, dark hair curled over the collar of her lab coat and she stood with both hands on her hips overseeing the excavation of Austin's latest John or Jane Doe. Between Chris and the river was a muddy area where the excavation was being carried out by three forensic technicians.

I walked down to the riverbank and stopped several feet to the left of Chris. A finger bone was pointed directly at me—well, not actually "pointing" per se, but it was sticking out of the mud and I happened to be in its path. A few inches down the bank, the curve of a pelvic bone emerged. The mud was sticky reddish-brown clay and the sole of my boots stuck in it and made a sucking sound as I pulled one foot up and stepped next to Chris.

Chris had an extensive background as a forensic anthropologist in addition to her work as a medical examiner. Because of that background, Chris understood why I liked to be in on a case as soon as possible. It helped me get a "feeling" for the victim and how he or she was murdered. She had awakened me at 5:30 a.m., given me the bare particulars and told me where to meet her. She stood there, intent on the riverbank, neatly dressed in a khaki skirt and a white button-down shirt with the white lab coat over her clothes. The sides of her shoes were caked with the red-brown mud that had curled up over the soles as Chris had made her way to the water's edge. At five-seven it seemed that I towered over Chris's five-foot-three stature. She looked over and up at me when I moved next to her.

"Nice outfit," she said sarcastically.

"When you wake me up at five-thirty in the morning to come to the river bottom to look at a body, don't expect me to dress up."

She smiled. "Actually I'm jealous. If I didn't have to go to the morgue and work a full day after this, I'd dress like that, too."

"How long do you think it'll take them to get the body out?"

"A while."

"That's accurate."

Chris gave me the eye roll.

"So, any idea of gender yet?"

"The skull is in pieces and there's not enough of the pelvis out of the mud yet. When there is, I can make an educated guess—although I'd prefer to do all that back in the morgue after I have all the bones."

"How long do you think the victim has been here?"

"Not as long as it has been dead."

"That's interesting, Chris, but I was really looking for something more specific."

Chris sighed, "Sorry. I'd say the person has been dead for years, but the bones have been here less than a couple of weeks. The City was doing some wastewater construction down here about a month ago and this would have been discovered then with all the equipment and digging..."

"So, are you saying this person was killed, buried somewhere else and then reburied here just a couple of weeks ago?"

"I'm not saying the body was ever buried anywhere, but it was definitely not buried here for long."

"Well now, that's a new twist. Not a very pretty twist, but it's new. How can you be so sure? Maybe the sewer crews weren't around this spot."

"It was a fresh grave and shallow. The bones we've uncovered weren't in the proper anatomical arrangement either and it isn't like the victim was dismembered. It's like someone just dumped them here in a hole, in a jumble."

"Nice. So, they dumped bones in the hole, in lieu of a body or body parts that decomposed here."

"Right. Also, I'd say the victim has been dead more than ten years—just guessing from the bones I've seen so far."

"Interesting."

"Yeah. Oh, as I said, the skull is in a few pieces, but we have it bagged and I'll put it together for you."

"Okay. Do you have most of the teeth?"

"Yes."

"Good, that'll help me with the reconstruct."

"It'll also help us make a positive ID when someone recognizes the victim from your artwork."

I nodded. "So, who are the cops on this one?"

"Your son and his partner. They're over on the other side of the road talking to the kayaker that found the body."

I decided to go see what Mike and Tommy were doing. I saw them talking to a young man dressed in a wet suit and reloading a kayak onto the top of his SUV. As I walked closer to them, they appeared to be leaving the man to his business and began to walk toward me.

My son, Mike Sullivan, was a homicide detective. He was tall, lean and wore his strawberry-blond hair cut short. Mike always wore a jacket and tie and nice shoes. He was a clean-cut, all-American-looking guy. His round, cherubic face belied his thirty years.

Mike's partner, Tommy Lucero, was a more senior detective and virtually Mike's polar opposite. Tommy always wore khakis with a button-down shirt open at the neck, western boots and no jacket. Tommy didn't wear a tie unless he was at a wedding or a funeral. He had been a rookie detective when my husband, Jack, was alive. He was ten years senior to Mike, but the difference in their appearances went beyond the ten-year age span.

Tommy was tall, but dark and muscular and chiseled in his body and facial features. He had an intensity that contrasted with Mike's mischievous humor, and a directness that counteracted Mike's avoidance of conflict. Mike's blue eyes sparkled with his good nature and Tommy's black eyes flashed with his passions. The things that would seem to make my son and his partner so incompatible were the very things that made them such a great team. Their strengths filled one another's weaknesses. Their friendship had made them the best homicide team in the department.

"So, what's the kayaker's story?" I asked.

"Discovered the bones this morning on his way up to the dam," Tommy said as he greeted me.

"On his way up to the dam?"

"Yeah, he and some other kayakers go up there to ride the waters that come through the floodgates," Mike explained.

"All this in spite of a sign right up there near the dam that specifically warns people not to do that."

"Yeah, well, there's nothing we can do to stop them," Tommy said. "Besides, this time one of them did us a favor by finding this person. Otherwise, spring rains come and they crank open three of those gates, and that whole area down there where he found the victim—all underwater."

"Bones washing down the river, Mom."

"Thank you for the graphic explanation, son. I was having trouble figuring that out for myself."

Tommy smiled and continued, "The guy was paddling by, saw the bones, got up close, saw they looked human and called 911 on his cell phone."

"We don't consider him to be a suspect," my son added.

"Well, since he looks like he's about twenty-one or twenty-two years old, I'd say you're right."

Mike furrowed his brow at me. "What does that have to do with anything?"

"Chris says the victim's been dead at least ten years, so the Crazy Kayaker would have been an adolescent at the time this person died. While it's possible that an adolescent can commit murder, I don't think it's probable under these circumstances."

"Why is it that you get all the good info before I do?"

"Because I ask, and because I hang out with the medical examiner."

"Mom, would you go sculpt something, please."

"You're just bent because you have to admit that Mom still knows something you don't know."

Mike gave me an eye roll and a sigh and Tommy started to laugh.

"Yeah, easy for you to laugh," my son said. "Your mom doesn't show up at crime scenes and bust your chops."

"No," Tommy said. "My mom waits until I come home for a nice Sunday dinner, and then she busts my chops."

"At least she's feeding you those killer tamales while she takes you down. By the way, she hasn't sent me any of those tamales lately—or has she, and you're just eating them all before I get any?"

Tommy smiled slyly and raised an eyebrow. "Hey, if you want any tamales, go see the woman in person and get your own. I'm not your errand boy."

"I haven't been invited. I was being polite."

"You don't need an invitation and you know it. My mom makes a bigger fuss over you than she does me. I have to go to your mom's house to get attention like that."

Mike looked at me. "You're feeding him and not inviting me?"

"Well, if you don't need an invitation at his mother's house, why would you need an invitation to come to your own childhood home? You can come over for dinner anytime you like."

"Yeah, whatever."

"You're awfully grumpy this morning, young man."

"Some of us had to get up early, shower and actually get dressed before we came down here," he said, giving my casual attire the once-over.

Tommy laughed again. "Hey, man, don't be dissing your mom like that. Toni's totally cool, and a pretty good-looking chick, if I may say so."

"Ick! You may *not* say so. This is my mom, and you're my partner. Besides, you have a girlfriend."

"I'm not dead, Mike. I may have a girlfriend, but I know a good-looking woman when I see one."

"Thank you, Tommy."

"You're totally welcome, Toni. You raised this guy?"

"Yes."

"Man, I would have thought you and Jack would have whipped more respect into him than this." Tommy smiled, thoroughly enjoying himself.

"He's had issues lately, I guess."

"Yeah, and my issue is, I'm the only guy on the force working homicides with my mom, and taking abuse from my partner simultaneously."

I smiled, patted my son on the arm and said, "You're such an abused child. Such a sad life."

I started walking back to the car.

Tommy laughed out loud.

"Later, Toni," Tommy yelled as I walked away.

I turned and waved as I got into the Mustang.

I stood at the back screen door, inhaling the fragrance of mountain laurel, redbud and ornamental peach blended by rainwater with the mustiness of oak and elm. It was three in the morning and the back of my neck was stiff from the five hours I had just spent reconstructing the face of a murder victim found near Hutto off of Highway 79. A thirtyish-year-old woman had been laid to rest in an untimely fashion in a grove of cottonwood trees. There she had spent the winter decomposing with the leaves, until two high-school kids hiked by and found her. Lieutenant Drew Smith of the Texas Rangers had asked me to put the woman's face back on her skull in the hopes that someone might recognize her. Without her identity, there was no hope of finding her killer.

I dug gray clay shavings out from under my fingernails and rolled my head back in a circular fashion to loosen the sore muscles. The half moon peeked between branches of new growth overhead and the soft, intermittent dripping of water from the eaves and trees hypnotized me into meditation in my fatigue. My eyes glazed over and I drifted back in time to a day I remembered working in the garage with my dad. The car was an old '50 Chevy that needed an oil change and the rain outside pounded down while Daddy instructed me on the finer points of removing and replacing an oil filter.

The phone rang like an alarm and I was startled out of my reverie. I hurried into the kitchen and picked up the receiver on the old black clunker on the wall.

"You sleepin', Toni?" an exhausted voice breathed.

"No, kid, I'm not. Sounds like you aren't either."

"Uh-uh," she groaned.

"So what're you doing about it?"

"Drank some hot tea earlier. Slept for a while. Been awake again now for an hour or so. What're you doin' up?"

My caller was one of the best fire investigators in the state. In her late thirties, Lieutenant Leonie "Leo"

Driskill had retired from "active combat" as a fire-fighter with the Austin Fire Department and now fought fires with her brain cells. She had a real knack for analyzing human behavior, too.

"I've spent the evening putting a face back on a dead gal," I said. "Started on it earlier today, gave it up for a while, went back to it about ten. I'm almost done now, but I think I'm gonna get some sleep here in a bit."

"You can do that? Just say I'm gonna go get some sleep and lie down and sleep comes?"

"Yep."

"Dead girl doesn't keep you awake after all that?"

"Nope. I'm trying to bring her some peace. I'm okay with that."

"Hmm. Got too many fires in my head, Toni. Can't put 'em out long enough to grab eight."

I knew it wasn't just fires keeping her awake, but she changed the subject back to my current recon-struction case, wanting to know more about the victim. I told her what we knew and then I men-tioned the bones found on Red Bud Isle the previ-ous morning. Leo was Tommy's girlfriend, but he had not mentioned the case to her. For all his teas-ing of Mike, Tommy had his own issues with a girl-friend who was as good an investigator as he was. I think if she had been in the police department in-stead of the fire department, their relationship might not have lasted. I thought Leo was actually better than either Tommy or my own son. Soon, I would request Leo to use her special insight into criminal behavior to help sort out the facts that would unfold in the coming days.

Chapter Two

The eyes are what haunt you—those beady, lifeless eyes, sculpted out of gray clay. I sculpted the "hair" out of clay as well. I would always sculpt a neutral style to the hair—short and combed for men, pulled away from the face for women. If the woman had short hair, the pulled-back style would mimic that. If the woman wore her hair long, she probably pulled it up or back from time to time, and again the style would be similar. Occasionally, there would be some hair left on a skeleton, or some article of clothing or a hair ornament that would give me a clue as to the actual appearance of the hair. In those instances, I would sculpt hair for the figure that I thought more accurately reflected the person's actual hairstyle.

There were several styles of forensic reconstructive art. There was the two-dimensional medium of charcoal and pencil drawings, which I used only in certain instances. There were sculptors who used glass eyes and actual wigs to finish their sculptures. There were sculptors who used fiberglass and other materials for sculpting. I liked to do most of my reconstructions in the three-dimensional medium of sculpture with pure clay. It wasn't better, it was just that I was more comfortable with it. I used plastics for making the molds, and plaster for casting the duplicated skulls, but the final result was just the clay. There was science in all the measurements that went into reapplying "flesh" to the skull, but the end result was a melding of that science with classical art. There seemed something more human about it all when I was finished.

My studio is a long room on one end of my house. There are windows on either end of the room—the front and back of the house. The ceiling is only nine feet—I prefer a twelve-foot one myself, but my house was what it was. Anyway, I have several tables in the room for various stages of my work and also for keeping busts that I've finished. There are some pedestals with work that I'd done purely for art, and I have a drafting board where I do sketches for all of my work.

I was in my studio finishing up my last case before beginning on the Red Bud victim, and I wondered who she was—this woman left to decompose among the cottonwood leaves. Her face was slim and oval-shaped. The nose bone was narrow and pronounced. It still had some of the cartilage on the very tip when she was found, although the buzzards had gotten just about all the other soft tissue. Her nose had a nice angular shape to it—a strong high ridge—and the brow formed a wonderful arch out of the nose and over the eyes. Her cheekbones were relatively high and created a smooth curve inward toward a narrow but rounded chin. The contrast of angles and curves gave her bone structure a delicate appearance overall.

In spite of the beauty I saw in this face, there was ugliness there, too. The ugliness was not hers, though. It was something inflicted upon her by human hands. There were scars—healed fractures in the bones of her face, and Drew said there had been similar scars in her arm bones and ribs.

The bone of her nose had also been broken, as had one of her cheekbones. Parts of her skull contained other fractures, too, but these wounds were not scars or healed breaks. These were death blows.

The face I had restored bore none of that terror. What I restored was a face made by the hand of God—a face that denied the abusive intervention of man. I blocked the horror of what I saw whenever I worked and remembered the sacred words: *"And God said, Let us make man in our image, after our like-*

ness... So God created man in his own image, in the image of God created He him; male and female created He them." As long as I could focus on what I was restoring, I didn't have to think about what had happened to the victim to put them in need of my skills.

With clay hair and eyes in place, the image was complete, and I placed it in the kiln for firing. When the bust was done, I removed it and set it out on one of my worktables. When it was cool, I made photos from all sides and then called Lieutenant Drew Smith at Ranger headquarters. He was in and wanted me to bring the bust over that day. It was a beautiful day for a drive through Austin. I put on my dark brown slacks, a short-sleeve beige sweater and my brown snakeskin boots. I placed the bust in a case for transport and loaded it into the Mustang.

It was cool and clear and a breeze blew through the trees and filled the air with the fresh green scent of spring. I rolled the windows down on the 'Stang and decided to take my scenic detour through town to get to Drew's office.

I lived in the older Hyde Park section of Austin and the trip to Ranger HQ should have been about fifteen minutes, but fifteen minutes didn't seem like enough time to enjoy all the sights and smells of the day, so I found my way to a road through the hills—to a road called Balcones.

The wind blew through my hair and I rode the curves all the way up Balcones as it wound its way above Lake Austin to a breathtaking view that I caught in my rearview mirror. I downshifted into second to make the rest of the grade, and looking forward, I made a left at the next intersection. Then I drove to the top of the mount, where I absorbed one of the best views in town.

Soon, I found my way back down, and made a right to head back into town toward Drew's shop. By the time I got there, it would be a thirty-minute trip, instead of the fifteen minutes of the more direct route, but these scenic detours were one of my favorite ways to avoid the gloom and doom that was inherent to the forensic work I did.

As I flew down and around the curves of the road, my thoughts turned to the face that would appear on the Red Bud Isle skull we had unearthed from the riverbank the previous morning. Once I was through with my meeting with Drew, I would have to call Chris and make arrangements to go down to the morgue for the casting of a mold of the skull. Once a mold had been made, I would take it back to my studio and begin the meticulous work of pouring a plaster version of the skull and fleshing it out with clay. What face would it reveal? The face of someone slain over ten years before, who had lain in a grave not only unidentified, but unmourned—a person whose fate had been utterly unknown for all that time. Whose face would it be? Who and where was the murderer now?

The road curved to the left and now I was on a straight path to Ranger headquarters. Within five minutes I approached the intersection at Lamar Boulevard, downshifted into second and wheeled the Black Beauty to the left, getting just a tad of tire squeal out of the rubber as I took the corner. A quick right turn into the parking lot and I was there, scoping for a place to land. I found a spot not too far from the front doors and made my way inside with case in hand.

It was always good to see Drew Smith. Drew and I had been friends a long time. We had met on a case years ago, and we had bonded as friends because our mothers were both from Terrebonne Parish in Louisiana. My mama's people were from Boudreaux and Drew's lived in Houma. My mom wasn't with us anymore, but Drew's Mama Beatrice, as everyone called her, was alive and kicking. She was some great lady. That woman could really cook, too. I had first met her on a trip back to Terrebonne Parish to visit some of my kin. She laid out a spread before me that would have fed five truck drivers. Then she insisted that I take leftovers home with me so I would have "something for the road." You could tell that Mama Beatrice was used to feeding three big boys, now three large men. Drew had a sister, too, but she was a petite thing like her mother, and I joked with her that she had remained small and slim because her brothers devastated the dinner table before she got anything to eat. She had laughed and said that there was too much truth in my joke.

Drew was a handsome African-American man who stood six feet, four inches tall, with square shoulders and a rock-solid body underneath them. He had a dazzling smile with an endearing overbite and the softest brown eyes I had ever seen in the face of a cop. He was between the ages of thirty-eight and forty, but he had old-fashioned manners and ethics, and that was a good thing in my book.

Make no mistake, however, Drew Smith was a law enforcement officer's law enforcement officer. True to the legend of the Texas Rangers, Drew got his man—or woman—and put them away. If he couldn't get them right away, he would dog a case until he finally dug up what he needed to make it stick. His work was meticulous and airtight every time—he made sure of it. He didn't tolerate sloppy work in others and he tolerated it even less in himself. You don't become a Texas Ranger by being average, and you don't become one of the best of the Texas Rangers by being anything other than excellent in law enforcement. For this reason, I always found it a true professional reward to work on a case with Drew.

Such was the case with the cottonwood victim. Drew would not let go of this seemingly hopeless case. He was an inspiration. He had insisted that I be brought in to do a reconstruct of the victim's face. Now I walked toward his office carrying the results of my work with me. A Jane Doe now had a face. Soon, she might also have a name. I knew that Drew Smith would not rest until he saw that she had both.

When I reached Drew's office, we shook hands and then hugged. I hadn't seen him in a month of Sundays. I set the case on his desk and slowly lifted the top off of it. When he saw the face he breathed in and out deliberately.

"Well, there she is then," he said. "Somehow I already knew her. This one has haunted me, Toni."

I nodded.

"I totally understand that. You should feel your hands in the clay, my friend."

He shook his head. "No, ma'am, I don't think I could do what you do. It's tough enough to do what I do."

He patted me on the back and smiled thoughtfully.

"Can I buy you a beverage?" he asked.

"No. I'm going to have to travel on to my next case."

"Another one already?"

"Unfortunately so. Bones by the river."

"Oh yes, yes. I read about it in the paper this morning. Sounds intriguing, Toni—very intriguing."

"I think I could stand a little less intrigue for a while."

Drew chuckled and then got out a Polaroid camera and made his own photos of the bust. He took the photos outside his office and handed them to a clerk, giving her instructions as to what to do with them. The photos would go out to all jurisdictions in Texas and various outlying jurisdictions in Louisiana, Oklahoma and New Mexico. All federal agencies would receive copies as well, and her face would make the six o'clock local news on all networks. Maybe someone would recognize her. Only then could anything be done about locating her killer.

I said goodbye to Drew, we hugged again and I left the building. As I walked back to my car, I turned and looked up at the window to Drew's office. I felt strange letting her go and leaving her there. I became attached to these anonymous persons. I wanted to care for her somehow, but I had done my best in that department by completing the bust. She was in good hands now. Drew would take care of her for me.

I called Chris from the car. She wanted to meet me for lunch down at Symphony Square, just a few blocks from the morgue. We would lunch on Tex-Mex before heading back to her office, where I could begin the first part of my work on our most recent victim. I only had to stop by the house briefly to pick up the supplies that I would need to make the mold. I took the short route to the house, picked up my things and headed downtown to meet Chris.

Chris was waiting at a table when I got there. She was dipping chips in hot sauce and wolfing them down as fast as her hand could make the trip from the basket to the bowl to her mouth and back to the basket again. I was always amazed to see someone so small and trim eating so much food. I wondered if she possessed a hollow leg.

"A little hungry today, are we?" I said as I took a seat opposite her.

"Mmm, hmm," she muttered with a chip in her mouth. "Another early morning *sans* breakfast. I've been a little busy trying to do an autopsy on those bones—and I'm not done yet."

"So, how goes the struggle?"

"Well, from one bone I discovered a type of soil that was inconsistent with the grave site—in other words, it was not that reddish-brown clay. It was embedded in one of the crevices of a bone—black, fertile-looking stuff. I found similar soil irregularities in other bones."

"So, the departed had been buried before."

"Mmm, hmm. Figured, but wanted to prove it."

"So what else?"

"Called a guy I know down at A&M and talked it all over with him. Told him I was sending him dirt samples. The samples are going down via the Mike Sullivan Express."

"Preserving the chain of evidence."

"Yep. Do you know those Aggies can almost pinpoint to the spot the origin of any soil in this state?"

"Doesn't surprise me. Agriculture is huge business here. If you're going to be an expert in ag, you have to know your dirt."

Chris nodded, still crunching chips. "Victim was a woman, I'd say probably between the ages of thirty and thirty-five at the time of her death."

"Race?"

"Caucasian."

"Know how she died yet?"

"Ordinarily that might take some careful scrutiny of the bones and I might come up with nothing, but in this case, an elementary schooler could have figured it out."

"The suspense is killing me—no pun intended—so give."

"Big bullet hole right in the skull," she said with a trigger finger pointed at her temple, firing with a thumb-hammer for emphasis.

"Nifty."

"Yep. I'm going to continue my review of the rest of the bones. If I find anything earth-shattering—no pun intended right back at you—I'll give you a shout."

"So you think she was shot ten years ago?"

"More. Ten years is the minimum. I'll have a better guesstimate of that when I'm done."

"Hmm."

"What?"

"I was just thinking...trying to remember what I might have been doing back then. Jack was still alive. My son was probably in high school. All that time gone by and she's lain dead and undiscovered."

"Yeah, someone shoots a woman in the head, buries her in one place and then comes back a few weeks ago, digs her up and buries her by the river. Very weird."

"Definitely weird. Why do you dig someone up and move their bones?"

"Don't know. Fetish?"

I shrugged. "I'd like Leo's take on this, though."

Leo Driskill was Chris's cousin by marriage. Leo's only living relative was her cousin, Pete Driskill, who was a brainy history expert. Pete and Chris had married about two years ago, making Chris and Leo cousins-in-law.

Chris nodded. "Call her."

The Travis County Morgue was only a few years old. The old morgue had been something out of a Charles Dickens novel and the county had finally popped to build a new one. New or not, morgues are the coldest places on earth, I think—all stainless steel with a mixture of smells that range from total disinfectant to malodorous death. It was never a great place to be, but it was a place I had to go to do the first stage of what I do.

Chris had put the skull back together for me and I saw the hole where the death wound had been inflicted. I wondered at who had ended this woman's

life in such a fashion. It was chilling to see it—this
broken skull pieced back together with that sinister
hole in the temple, and to envision in my mind the
living person receiving such a wound. In my mind I
could see before me the woman with flesh on the
bones, and I drifted to that moment of death. The
barrel of the gun was against her temple, she was
terrified, overcome with disbelief that this was her
last moment. A finger squeezed the trigger, then
there was the thunder of the hammer hitting the firing pin, and the explosive impact of the bullet. I
shuddered and snapped back into the current reality.

"Are you okay?" Chris asked.

"Yes. I was just thinking about how she died."

Why had she been reburied so long after her
death? It was a new one on me, and I couldn't imagine what was going on, but I knew that my work
would be critical to finding the answers. Identification of the victim is the most important stage in a
murder like this.

I began to mix the materials I needed to make a
mold of the skull. I had my own technique for this
process. I used a plastic material similar to the one a
dentist uses for making impressions of teeth. The
skull is impressed into the material, and then the material hardens to a certain point, at which time I re-
move the skull. I then take the mold back to my
studio and cast it in plaster. Once the plaster is dry,

I begin sculpting the clay face back to life on the plaster skull.

When I had this skull in the casting phase, Chris showed me the rest of the bones that had been recovered from Red Bud Isle.

"We found all of them, so wherever she was buried before, she was undisturbed, and the killer moved her entire skeleton."

I nodded and looked at all the bones neatly arranged in their proper anatomical order—a now-headless skeleton laid out on a cold autopsy table.

"Were there any personal effects found?"

"Yes."

I looked at her quizzically.

"Just this." She pointed to one corner of the table.

It was a tattered piece of what appeared to be flowered cloth.

"Clothing?"

Chris nodded. "Probably part of a dress or blouse."

"So, assuming she was originally buried with clothes, the clothes either decomposed completely, except for this scrap, or the killer discarded those and retrieved only the bones but missed this scrap."

"That would be about the size of it. There were no other personal effects, so I'd say the killer ditched them all."

"There's another happy thought. How long before the Aggies have results on the soil samples?" I asked.

"They didn't give me a time frame, but they have to analyze the samples for mineral content and all the little microbes they find there, so I imagine it'll take a little bit anyway. Between your reconstruction of her face, and their location of the burial soil, we might actually get lucky enough to figure this out."

"I hope you're right."

After I left the morgue, I tried Leo at her office, but the woman who answered the phone said that Lieutenant Driskill was in the field. So, I called her on her cell phone. When she picked up, I could tell she was in transit.

"So, you're out in the field following up on hot leads?"

"That's a glamorous way of putting it. I just got through interviewing a rent-a-cop that I think might be suffering from a little firebug."

"Seriously?"

"Unfortunately so. He has all the signs and he fits the behavior pattern. I got him to write out the facts of a fire he 'reported.' I'm taking the written description to a psychologist for analysis right now."

"Wow. Well, I'm calling you because Chris and I would like to talk to you about the bones from Red Bud Isle."

"Okay. Something there for me to work with?"

"It's not the original burial place and there was a large bullet hole in the skull."

"Interesting. When I get done with my forensic psychologist, I'll go by the morgue and get the details from Chris. I'll let you know if I come up with anything brilliant."

"So, what's up with this rent-a-cop case?"

"Warehouse fire. Fire was definitely started by human hands and not an accident. Three security guards, one killed."

"Oh no, that's terrible! Did he burn to death?"

"No. Smoke inhalation, or more exactly, toxic-fume inhalation, combined with soot and searing heat. It's actually what kills most people in a fire."

"Who's the homicide detective on it?"

"Tommy and your son. They suspect the other guard. I know he's innocent. The guard I'm working on is the guy who did it. I'm going to make sure an innocent man doesn't go down. Tommy hates it when I do this, but that's tough. I'm going to do my job in spite of any personal relationships I have with the homicide team. I'll tell you more when I come by with an assessment of your Red Bud case."

"Good. I'd like to hear more."

Inside my studio, I mixed plaster and poured it into the mold I had made of the skull when I was down at Chris's office. The process was familiar, but never tedious or routine. I always approached my work with the reverence it was due. I was making a cast of someone's skull—the skull of a person who had been deprived of her life in a cruel and untimely way. My subjects were always real people who had real families and friends. They were flesh and bone, and spirit in my beliefs—and while temporarily separated, they were all parts of a whole and real person. I never forgot that in my work.

When the plaster dried, I would open the synthetic mold and begin restoring her face. As I let the plaster set, I began my preparation. I lit a candle and I began to pray. Her soul would be at peace soon— I wanted it to be at peace with a name attached to it. I prayed, as I always did, for the guidance to do this right.

Chapter Three

The skull looked as if it was covered with pencil erasers. They were tissue-depth indicators, actually, and had been cut precisely to a depth for each portion of the face, based on statistics from a forensic anthropology chart. I had taken the basic information of race, gender and approximate age to decide which part of the chart to use. Now it looked as though her skeleton had some strange version of the measles. My next step would be to fill in between the indicators with clay, the top of each indicator showing me where to stop and smooth it off. It was like connect the dots for sculpture, although I would have to use my sculpting skills to make the raw, three-dimensional "data" look like a real human being. I was intently focused on my work, when the phone rang. I was so startled, I nearly fell off my stool.

I picked up the cordless handset that I had carried into the studio and was surprised to hear Irini Nikolaides on the other end of the line, distress in her voice. We exchanged the normal greetings of good friends before she broke the news.

"Toni, they may have found my Teddy's bones in that horrible jungle."

Stunned, I sat unable to form a thought, much less a word. Theodore Nikolaides had been a good friend to my husband and me in the Vietnam War. In fact, it was Ted, my compadre in faith, who had introduced me to Jack. "He's a nice guy for you, Toni," Ted had said—the matchmaker concerned that this woman serving in a battle zone should find a proper husband. I was a nurse then, helping put young boys back together hoping to send them home alive. Jack had been an MP there.

Teddy had talked to Jack about faith because of me. Jack hadn't attended church in years and didn't have any particular religious preference at the time. Ted thought he'd be a good match for me, but only if we could share faith with each other. Ted could talk to him about it—share his own experiences with Jack man-to-man. When Jack and I actually met, Jack's conversations with Ted about faith were already taking hold. He had embraced his faith with his whole heart again and he and I had made a beautiful journey together in our lives.

Unfortunately, our matchmaker had not made the journey with us. As a pilot, Teddy flew reconnaissance missions close over the jungle treetops. One terrible day he flew out on what should have been his last mission before heading home. His hitch was up and he couldn't wait to get back stateside with his wife and two kids. He was so excited. I could still remember that magnetic smile as he boarded his plane.

Then the word came back that Ted had been shot down and no ejection or chute had been seen. Other pilots reported seeing his plane crash on the top of a hill. It had skidded along a ridge with dense foliage. I knew that Ted, ever the hero, was trying to save himself and the plane. Determined not to give up, he must have struggled to keep the nose up and wings in the air, but it was too late to eject as he came close to the hilltop. So, Ted had committed himself to trying to land the plane. The wings had broken off as the plane began hitting trees, and then it had burst into flame. It wasn't a spectacular fire because Ted was at the end of his mission and low on fuel, but it had been enough to ensure his death.

"Irini, what are we talking about here?"

"Those people at CILHI, they sent a team to that part where Teddy was last seen. They found bones and some other things and they think it might be him."

CILHI stands for Central Identification Laboratory Hawaii, and they are the ID people for all military personnel missing in action. It's an army operation located at an air force base just outside of Honolulu. They work to identify all MIAs from World War II, Korea and Vietnam.

"When will they know if it's him?" I asked.

"Well, that is why I called you. They won't know because there are not enough of the teeth to compare to Teddy's dental records. You know, he had such good teeth, but they check the bad ones in these tests, not the good ones, and most of Ted's teeth they didn't find. So, now they can't do the comparison. Also, the DNA is bad."

"What do you mean?"

"They say they have to compare it to someone in his mother's family."

Ted's mother had died in Greece. His father had brought him and his brother with him after she died. His mother had one brother back in Greece and they had lost track of him after World War II during the civil war that followed. Ted had talked about it many times. The only family he knew was his father's family. Further complicating matters was the fact that Ted's older brother, and only sibling, had a heart attack four years previously and died.

Irini continued, "I ask them why they don't check it with someone else in his family or against the kids.

They say it's not the right kind of DNA. I don't understand it."

"It's called mitochondrial DNA, Irini. It can only be compared against a person's mother's family. The other kind of DNA in your cells breaks down over time, so they probably can't use it."

"I don't know anyone in Ted's mother's family. They left the uncle behind in Greece and we don't know what happened to him."

"I know. I remember."

"Toni, the skull is good. They can't use the DNA there for nothing, but I talked to them about you and they say they have worked with you twice before. They say because you work for the FBI sometimes, they use you for help."

"That's true, but what are you saying, Irini?"

"I am saying that you must help me and Teddy. You must go and make a sculpture of this skull and put the face there, so we can see if it is Teddy."

"Irini, this is difficult work when I don't know the victim, but..."

"No. His soul is restless. He cannot be at peace until they give me his bones and let me lay him to eternal rest. They will not give me the bones until they know it is him. The peace of his soul is with you, Toni. You must do this for him—to restore him, to bring him home, to set him free."

I had a knot in my stomach and I was beginning to feel sick. The war had been put behind me. Jack and I had used our faith to heal us from the things that happened there, including the loss of our beloved friend, Ted. I hated it, but what Irini was saying was right. What she wasn't saying was that I owed this to Ted because of his friendship to me and for bringing me to Jack. I had a great marriage for all those years, and Irini had lived alone, raising their children and having no closure over the death of the only man she had ever loved. I sighed. My chest felt tight.

"They have the skull, all of it?"

"Yes," she said. "All of that part of the bones are in good shape. The rest they say is bad, but you don't need the rest to make the face."

"Okay, give me the name of the person in charge so I can call and set this up."

There was a momentary silence on the other end of the phone. I heard the rustling of some paper, and then, choking back tears, Irini read the name and phone number to me of the man at CILHI who was in charge of "Ted's case."

She could barely speak when we hung up, but her last words to me were, "May our Savior bless you and guide your hands."

I was noodling around in the garage with an old carburetor, trying to work through my angst, when I heard a vehicle pull to the curb and stop in a hurry. When Lieutenant Leonie Driskill drove her official vehicle, a rather cumbersome van loaded with equipment, she drove like the law enforcement officer that she was. When Leo got behind the wheel of her Jeep, tires would screech and squeal.

She bailed out of the Jeep with her sandy hair swinging in a ponytail down her back. She had just gotten off work. She was still wearing navy trousers and a white shirt, and her badge and gun were clipped to her belt. She was about five-five and she walked with a slight limp from her last fire battle in active combat. It had almost cost her her right leg. The doctors had said she probably wouldn't walk and definitely wouldn't be able to do anything more physical than that. No one ever told Leo Driskill she couldn't do something without her trying that much harder. She had rehabbed her way back to health and extreme fitness. She lifted weights and ran and water-skied, and proved the doctors wrong.

Her limp gave her just a little bounce when she walked fast, and today there appeared to be an extra spring in her step besides the limp.

"What are you working on out here, Toni?"

"Just a carburetor overhaul on my old Jeep." I wiped some of the grease off my hands with a rag and headed for the Go-Jo canister. I smeared Go-Jo all over my hands, loosening all the grease, and then wiped my hands clean with a dry rag.

Leo sauntered over to the workbench and started to inspect the carburetor.

"Touch that and you'll be sorry."

"I-eeee...wasn't..." Her voice trailed off as if she'd been caught with her hand in the cookie jar.

"I just spent half an hour getting all those needles lined up just right so I could get that thing back together," I told her. "You knock it over or mess it up and your name is mud."

I turned around to see that Leo was leaning over the workbench with her hands behind her back, eyeing the carburetor closely. She looked like a heron perched on a log.

"You know, Toni, most people take stuff like this to a mechanic."

"Yeah well, four things are true, kid. Most people don't have a mechanic for a dad. Most people weren't practically raised in a garage. Most people don't know a thing about carburetors, and I'm not most people."

"That's the truth—the 'you're not most people' part, anyway."

"Are you here to harass me and disturb my auto-mechanican therapy session or do you have something important you'd like to impart?"

"Grump. You call me in the middle of my busy day and ask me to go look at a bunch of old bones dug up out of the river bottom, and when I come by to give you the benefit of my report, this is how I'm treated."

I sighed. "Truce already. I can't spar with you anymore today."

"Hey, lighten up. I was kidding. What gives?"

"It's just been a bad day. It has to do with old times in Vietnam. I'll work it out. Distract me by giving me your brilliance on our Red Bud case."

Leo nodded. "I'm afraid there's no brilliance yet. There's not much I can say because there's not much to go on. But there were a few things that came to mind based on the apparent cause of death and the reburial."

"Lay it on me."

"Well, I looked at the photos of the burial site and I looked at the bones themselves and talked to Chris about the autopsy. I definitely tanked any idea that they were moved because someone thought they'd be discovered where they were. I think it's significant that they were reburied in a shallow grave on the dam side of Red Bud. According to the photos, the bones were in a place where they would have washed away in the first floodgate release. The kayaker was the unknown quantity that foiled that plan."

"Okay, so why do you think they were reburied and not just discarded—thrown into the river, for instance."

"I think the fact that isn't what happened is very significant. I think the deceased either meant something to the killer and he couldn't do that, or maybe he felt too much guilt to do that, or maybe a little of both. I suspect he wanted to be rid of her, but he wanted nature to do the ultimate dirty work so he wouldn't be responsible for it."

"So, why dig her up and try to get rid of her after all this time?"

"That's the twenty-five-thousand-dollar question. Something changed in the killer, or something else happened that caused him to dig her up and move her like that. He may have just wanted to be rid of the memory of it, or it could have been a combination of things that happened at once. When we figure that out, we'll have all the answers."

"What about the way she was killed? You said you thought she might have meant something to the killer, but it looks to me like he just executed her."

"I think he did, but that doesn't mean she didn't mean something to him. In fact, he had more of a reason to kill her if she meant something to him. He may have even planned it out in his mind before."

"Elaborate."

"Maybe the killer believed she did something to him for which she deserved to be 'executed'—and it's possible that the deceased may not have even actually committed the offense for which she was killed."

"What do you mean?"

"I mean that if the killer was paranoid, which is totally possible, and thought she did something to deserve being killed, then he probably thought about killing her for a while. It satisfied the paranoid

feelings he had. In fact, it may all be in his mind anyway, and we may find in the end that this victim
didn't even do what the killer thought she did. This
kind of killer would kill for some offense with or
without any real proof, based solely on what he believed, because he convinced himself in his mind
that it's absolutely true, that someone is to blame,
and he believed that the person deserved to pay."

"That's interesting. What gives you the impression the killer might be this kind of killer?"

"The way she was killed seems calculated and or-
ganized and I don't see any passion in it. The lack of
passion leads me to believe that he thought she deserved this in some way. In other words, it wasn't
done spur of the moment—thought went into it.
Hence the execution style to the shooting. But this
burial and reburial and what I see in that isn't orga-
nized or thought out at all in my opinion—and he reburied her in a way that he wouldn't be responsible
for discarding her remains. It's completely irrational.
Plus, in my gut I feel that his attempt to discard her
is part of his denial of guilt and that goes hand in hand
with this kind of personality—'Someone else is to
blame in all this, not me. She deserves all of this.'"

"So, in a nutshell, he thinks she's done something
to him and he kills her. He plans the killing, but then
later his actions—the reburial—are committed in
response to some other event?"

"Right."

"This helps a lot."

"It's all just my impression—a gut feeling at this point—based on an execution-style bullet hole and bones dumped and carelessly reburied in a shallow grave. I just let it run through my head and try to see the event the way it might have happened. Then I try to imagine why the person would have done the murder that way. What was his motive in carrying out these actions?"

I smiled. It was the way I worked a crime scene—letting it run through my mind, but I didn't have the knowledge of behavior that Leo had, just an eye for detail.

"Anything else?" I asked.

"Nope. Just keep me in the loop, because now I'm tantalized." She smiled broadly.

"Oh, one more thing."

"Yeah?"

"We both have been referring to the killer as 'he.' Any chance the killer is a woman?"

"Sure. I was just using the 'he' in a more general sense, but a woman could have all the same issues and could be the killer. I'll tell you, though, the statistics say it's more likely to be a guy."

"I hope my work sheds more light on it all."

"Your work usually does, Toni."

"I've already started the bust."

"Good. So, got any root beer in this place?" Leo grinned.

"Brat. Come on inside and we'll drink the best root beer anywhere."

We went into my kitchen and I pulled two ice-cold IBC root beers out of the fridge. IBC is bottled in Plano, and it's genuine old-fashioned Texas root beer. I grabbed two frosted mugs from the freezer and poured the soda down the sides of each mug for minimum suds.

"Let's drink these on the patio. What do you say?"

"You're twisting my arm, Toni."

We sat down in the Adirondack chairs I had outside and got into a relaxed mode. I took a long, slow swallow of the bubbly stuff.

"Ahh, this is the best."

"You know how to serve root beer, Toni."

"Well, I've had a little experience."

"So, what's up with grumpiness and carburetor overhauls and Vietnam?"

I sighed and told her about Ted and the phone call from Irini.

"You know, I forget that you were in 'Nam," she said. "You almost never talk about that. I even forget that you were a registered nurse."

"When I came back from Vietnam I wanted to forget I was a registered nurse, too."

"So, you got into forensics?"

"Well, it didn't happen like that. I went back to school and got my art degree, then my master's and

Ph.D. It was a fluke that I got into this line of work. It used to not exist, you know."

"Yeah, I guess that's right."

"I got into it because of Jack's work as a detective, and my love of and involvement in art, particularly in sculpture."

"That makes sense."

We both took another long swallow of root beer and sat in silence for a few minutes.

"So, Toni, what was 'Nam like?"

"Blood and bombs and horrible smells—gasoline and jet-fuel smell in everything—and death, lots of death."

"I guess you saw some terrible stuff."

"Yes, I did, but I was a triage nurse for flying wounded boys to other hospitals or home, so I didn't see the worst of it. The army nurses out in the field saw things I think would have driven me mad."

"I've seen some pretty bad stuff in fires. I can't imagine going to war like that. So, you and Jack just hung out with Ted most of the time?"

"When we were all off duty we did. There was this place there—just a dump where we ate and hung out. We'd spend hours there yucking it up and talking about how great it would be when we all got back home."

"Wow. I'm sorry, Toni."

"Yeah, it makes me sick sometimes. Ted never made it, and now Jack's gone. It'd be a lot easier to handle Ted being found if Jack was still here with me. It really stinks."

"I'm in touch with that emotion in a big way."

Now I felt really bad. Here I was talking about all this to Leo, and her parents and brother were all dead, and her only living relative was her cousin, Pete. Her parents had been killed by a drunk driver on 2222, and her brother, formerly Tommy Lucero's partner, had been shot to death in the line of duty just over a year ago.

"I'm sorry, kid, I wasn't thinking."

"Aw, don't start walking on eggshells around me. I don't own grief, you know. Vietnam was horrible. I'm sure Ted wasn't the only person you knew there who didn't make it. You have a right to feel what you feel about that."

"Unfortunately, Ted *wasn't* the only friend we had there who didn't make it. He was the friend we knew and loved the most, I guess, but there were so many others. Oh man, marines there on the base who went off on patrol and they'd come back with a third of the guys gone, and two or three of those were friends of ours. Pilots that flew off and never came back—it was an endless stream."

"So now Ted may have been found, and you have to help figure that out."

"Yes."

"And that takes you right back into the endless stream again."

"Yeah."

"I totally understand. Toni?"

"Yes."

"You can talk to me about it anytime. Sometimes it's better to talk about these things with someone who gets it. Know what I mean?"

"Yeah, kid, I do."

❧ *Chapter Four* ❧

Sergeant Major Tomlinson called me back from the CILHI labs in Hawaii. CILHI's staff includes thirty anthropologists, four forensic odontologists (dentists) and numerous other forensic scientists. They also employ other experts on an as-needed basis, which can include any legitimate expert requested by the family of a missing service person. I had been used twice previously to reconstruct the faces of two servicemen recovered from Laos and Cambodia.

The Sergeant Major remembered me. With his typical military courtesy, he continually addressed me as "Dr. Sullivan" because of my Ph.D. in art. It made me uncomfortable. I had worked hard to complete my formal education, but I considered the informal education of my life's experiences to be more important, and that education had been completed by "Toni," not Dr. Sullivan.

We spoke about my phone conversation with Irini. He was familiar with the case and gave me all the details from his perspective.

It had been a long road to find remains that might actually belong to Teddy. Three times before, CILHI had thought they would bring Ted home. The first time, they dug at a site they thought was near his supposed crash site, but they found nothing. They conducted more interviews with the locals and continued searching for the right site.

The second time they were supposed to go in and search a site, there were political problems and they weren't allowed in. The third time, with political problems resolved, they went in to search the second site and labored again with no results.

More interviews with locals and more research had pointed them to this new site. Here they had found fragments of bones, pieces of the airplane— some parts of it had been cannibalized by the locals for use in homemade farming equipment—and they also found other personal items that had definitely belonged to a U.S. serviceman. They sifted the soil in that location for months and collected everything they could find. Now they just needed a way to prove that what they had found were the remains of Captain Theodore P. Nikolaides.

As Irini had said, few teeth were recovered and the ones they found were only Ted's good teeth and not the ones they needed to make a positive match to his dental work. The nuclear DNA had deteriorated, but that was expected. The mitochondrial DNA was totally usable, but there was no one with whom they could compare it. They had used that DNA, however, to match the bone pieces and the skull—that was a match. Knowing that all those parts belonged to the same person meant that once the ID had been made through my facial reconstruction, all the matching pieces could be said to belong to someone—he would have a face, a name, a history and a family and friends.

If these were Ted's remains, he would get a posthumous Purple Heart and qualify for burial in Arlington National Cemetery. His family would have closure and his fellow American citizens would lay him to rest with full military honors. It seemed a cheap price for the life of such a man and it was long overdue, but it was more than a man like Ted Nikolaides would have ever expected or asked for his service. But then, that is the hero's way and my friend Ted had been a hero long before he ever gave his life for his country.

Sergeant Major Tomlinson and I agreed that I would arrive in Honolulu at Hickham Air Force Base next week to begin my work. I would make my own travel arrangements.

* * *

It was three in the morning. I sat on the patio behind my house, barefoot, wearing my jeans and a
pullover sweatshirt, with a mug of root beer in my
hand. I was slumped down in an Adirondack chair
gazing up at the stars and the elliptical track above
me. I had picked out a couple of planets, but couldn't
remember which one was Mars and which one
Venus. My brain was otherwise occupied and all
other data had slipped off-line.

Teddy Nikolaides had great teeth and a brilliant
smile to show them off. His smile was broad, engag-
ing and completely sincere—consequently, it was absolutely mesmerizing. It was painful at this point to
remember the joy of that smile.

*The last day I saw Ted was supposed to be his last
day in Vietnam, not his last day on this side of life. The
weather had been incredible that day. Ted had orders
to go home. He was supposed to leave for Saigon and
then go on to Hawaii, where he would change planes
and continue back to the mainland—to Chicago. There
he would be with his beautiful Irini and their two children, Eleni and Gregory. Eleni was four and Gregory
was almost two.*

*From the moment he got up that day, Ted had been
more energetic than usual. He had been jubilant. He
had to fly one more mission and it was supposed to be
a short one, and then he was leaving. Before he
boarded the plane, he had come to say goodbye to*

Jack and me. He wasn't sure there would be time when he got back before he headed off for Saigon. The three of us talked of Ted's trip home, of how Jack and I would get together with Ted and Irini in the States, and of all the incredibly good times we knew the four of us would have together. Ted was talking of moving his family from Chicago to Texas. He and Irini had already discussed it. Irini and I had talked on the phone and began to write one another. She wanted to move, to live in a place that was more like her home country.

As the three of us finished our conversation, there was a moment where sorrow almost overcame us, but Ted wouldn't allow it.

"No tears," he had said. "There will be such good times for all of us, and it will be soon."

We all hugged and laughed as Ted made jokes. He walked out to his plane and climbed on board, pulled on his helmet and raised his hand high in one final greeting, beaming his beautiful joyous smile.

I tilted the mug over my lip and let the carbonated beverage flow in a long swallow. It was my second glass. In spite of the hour, I was seriously considering a third. After the two reconstructs I had done for CILHI, I knew what to expect in terms of remains. The skulls I had worked on previously had been put together from pieces—lots of pieces. The one on which I would do the reconstruct this time was only in five pieces. The forensic anthropologist had put them back together already. Apparently, the only reason there were pieces of the skull to reconstruct was due to some fluke of protection that had been offered by the pilot's helmet, and the nature of the crash.

All that was left were just pieces of bones, bones of those long dead—dry bones.

I laid my head back against the chair and whispered, "Dry bones..."

I thought about death and life, about dry bones and prophecies of resurrection and the words of the prophet Ezekiel flowed into my mind: *"The hand of the Lord was upon me, and carried me out in the spirit of the Lord, and set me down in the midst of the valley which was full of bones, and caused me to pass by them round about: and, behold, there were very many in the open valley; and, lo, they were very dry..."*

They were very dry—a symbol for those long dead.

The prophet continues, *"Thus saith the Lord God unto these bones; Behold, I will cause breath to enter into you, and ye shall live.. and the breath came into them, and they lived, and stood up upon their feet, an exceeding great army...behold they say, Our bones are dried, and our hope is lost: we are cut off for our parts... Thus saith the Lord God; Behold, O my people, I will open your graves, and cause you to come up out of your graves...and shall put my spirit in you and ye shall live, and I shall place you in your own land..."*

Place you in your own land...

The dead lie on the jungle floor for thirty years or more and what's left by the time they are discovered and brought home is a pretty disheartening sight. The recovery teams mark off the supposed "burial" sites like archaeological digs. They trowel slowly and carefully within the dig and "exhume" each and every little piece of anything that looks as if it might have belonged to a human or one's body. They tag everything, bag everything and ultimately bring it back to American soil. They bring it all back to the U.S. Army CILHI labs at Hickham Air Force Base in Hawaii. There, forensic anthropologists, forensic odontologists, DNA lab technicians and, sometimes, forensic artists come together to help identify the remains of the missing. We are all the new undertakers of the post-Vietnam era. You don't need a real undertaker just to put "rocks" in a box. Sadly, that's what most of the remains look like.

That was what was eating at me now—rocks in a box. Now they might be someone I knew. It's one thing to put your hands on the skull and bones of a stranger and try to ID them and bring them some level of peace, and their families some level of closure, but it is something else altogether to contemplate placing your hands on a skull that may have housed the thinking brain of a friend—a skull that held his eyes, ears, mouth and the nose through which he breathed the breath of life itself.

Teddy Nikolaides used to tilt his head back and laugh out loud with absolute joy. Did the skull I would cast in Hawaii once reverberate with that laughter? The burden of determining that answer now lay solely with me. If I determined the remains belonged to someone else, it would be a huge blow to me and to Teddy's family. If I determined the remains belonged to Teddy, we would all have to deal with the reality of his death. Since that fateful day in Vietnam, his death had not been confirmed in any tangible way. There had been no real closure. He just flew off one day and never came back. I sighed and polished off the rest of the root beer that was in the bottom of my mug. I had another frosted mug in the freezer and it was time for a third.

It was early morning, when I was startled awake by the word "Mom!"

I looked up to see the sun filtering through the low-hanging branches of my backyard. Initially, I couldn't remember where I was or what I was doing there. The first thing I realized was that my feet were cold. Then I realized there was a tall, strawberry-blond man standing over me, but I couldn't see his face due to all the backlighting from the sun. He was wearing a gun in a holster that hung on his belt and the sunlight glinted off of a gold detective's badge. I recognized my son's voice, and then I remembered where I was and what I was doing there.

"I was beginning to wonder if I was going to have to get the smelling salts."

I shielded my eyes with my hands and squinted so I could see his face.

"What are you talking about?"

"I thought maybe you had some kind of spell."

"Don't be smart. I just fell asleep."

"Well, how many 'mature' women spend the night on the patio sleeping on an Adirondack? Then there are all these mugs and bottles..."

"Root beer, smarty, and you know it."

He was chuckling now and enjoying every minute of it.

"I'm sure you've never done anything like this," I said as I struggled to sit up straight and regain part of my dignity.

"Mario, you're not looking so speedy this morning."

I backhanded him in the leg.

"Watch your mouth."

Mario was his nickname for me—after Mario Andretti. I had acquired this moniker on account of my love for a fast car with a stick shift and an open road on which to drive it. Sometimes my right foot would become very heavy, especially if the road was *really* open.

He chuckled. "So, what's the occasion?"

"I had a bad afternoon yesterday. What are you doing here so early anyway?"

"I came by to see what kind of progress you were making on the bust of our Red Bud victim."

"I was working on it, and then Irini called."

"Theia Irini?"

He used the Greek word in referring to his "Aunt Irene." Irini had been our close friend since before Michael was born, and he had grown up with her around and being a part of our extended family in faith. She was his godmother. He had learned to speak some Greek, too, and he did a pretty good job.

"Yes," I said.

"What's wrong? Is Greg okay?"

Greg was one of Mike's best friends.

"Gregory is fine."

"What then?"

I sighed and put my head in my hands, running my fingers through my short, graying red hair. I looked up at Michael.

"CILHI thinks it has Ted's remains."

Mike sank into the chair next to me.

"Wow."

We looked at each other.

"So, what's the rest, Mom?"

"Not enough teeth for a dental ID and nothing to compare the DNA with, but the skull is in decent enough shape."

Mike looked down at the ground between his feet.

"Whew." He paused a moment and then looked over at me. "So, what're you going to do?"

"Well, I've committed to it. I have to, no matter how I feel about it."

Mike nodded. He reached over and squeezed my right shoulder. "It's the right thing, Mom. Anything I can do?"

"Be here."

"You got it."

We sat there a moment in silence.

"Hey, Mom?"

"Yeah."

"I can't believe you fell asleep on one of these hard wood chairs."

"Hey, Mike?"

"Yeah."

"I fell asleep on one of these hard wood chairs."

"Thanks, Mom."

"You're welcome."

๛ Chapter Five ๛

After my little campout on the patio, I decided I needed to get my rear into gear before I was going to be able to get my head together. One of the rooms in my house is set aside as a weight room with a bench and rack and a couple of machines for back and leg work, a roman chair for abs and low back and a pulley set up for more arm and chest work.

I suited up in my black cotton sweatpants and racer-back top and did a fifteen-minute warm-up on the recumbent stationary bike. Thoroughly warmed up, I did a full set of stretches and hit the weights. I hadn't been in the gym for days, so I went at it hard, doing a full-body workout, supersetting everything for maximum cardio benefit. When I was done with that, I got back on the recumbent bike and did another thirty minutes.

I was dripping in sweat when I was done, but I felt a hundred percent better—mentally and physically. I got into a steaming-hot shower and washed everything out of my system—at least temporarily.

Refreshed from my exercise and hot shower, I put on a clean pair of jeans and socks, a white cotton T-shirt and my favorite pointy-toed boots and went to the studio.

I sat on the stool in front of my drafting table and began to make a list of everything I would need to take with me to Hawaii. I would need a case in which to carry the cast I would make of the skull. I began to list other tools and supplies to pack.

I sat back and took a deep breath. Who was I kidding? What I would need most of all was the spiritual fortitude to face this task and all that it meant to me. I would need that to go back into the jungles of Vietnam in my mind.

I set my pen down on the drafting board and got the phone instead. It was time to call Reverend Iordani. I needed to walk and talk.

When Jack died from a sudden and unexpected heart attack six years ago, my world came apart like a house of cards. Reverend Iordani used to walk with me along the riverbank under the cypress trees. I don't remember much of it. Life for me then existed in a fog, but I remembered the cypress trees and their peaceful effect.

I sat on a bench under the great spreading branches of one of those peaceful trees and waited. True to form and ten minutes late—they call it Greek time—Reverend Iordani came strolling down a grassy bank that led from the street to the trail along the river. He beamed at me and waved.

I got up and began to walk toward him. I kissed his hand and then we greeted in the traditional Greek way with the exchange of three kisses. As we began to walk, we talked about my two most recent cases: the woman under the cottonwoods and the one just discovered upriver on Red Bud Isle. Reverend Iordani listened carefully, complimented me on my hard work and efforts and asked me about Mike.

Then he stopped under a large tree and said, "Toni, this isn't why you called me, so tell me what this is really about."

"Irini called me the other day. They think they've found Ted's remains in Vietnam."

The reverend knew all about Ted. Irini lived just outside of town in Dripping Springs, and she came to our church. He knew Irini well.

"Wow," he almost whispered. He said, "May his memory be eternal."

He had a hushed sound to his voice—a peaceful, calm demeanor. All of this was part of his normal way, but now it was more pronounced.

"They can't make a positive ID on his remains for a lot of reasons, but there's enough of the skull for a reconstruct," I told him.

"That's the only way they'll know for sure?"

I nodded and looked down at my feet, making curlicue shapes in the dirt with the tip of my boot.

The reverend raised his eyebrows, stroked his close-cut beard and said simply, "I see."

We made our way to a bench a few feet down the trail. Reverend Iordani's counsel had helped me heal many wounds—wounds from 'Nam, wounds from difficult cases and wounds from Jack's death. The reverend was twenty years younger than me and still raising his children, but he had spiritual wisdom, and it was wisdom I needed right now. We sat and began to talk about what I had been told about Ted's remains. When I had finished with all of it, the reverend took another deep breath.

"Well, of course you have to do it," he said.

I nodded. "I know that, but I need help to get through it. To go to Vietnam again, so to speak."

He nodded. "Toni, you're a spiritual person. I know you read the scripture and keep a strict rule of meditative prayer. I also know that you read the works of the spiritual fathers and continue to expand your knowledge of our faith, but there's one thing I notice about you lately."

I waited a moment for him to gather his thoughts.

He spoke slowly and softly, "All the work you do is great work. Your work is bringing peace to a lot of people and their relatives who are still on this side of life, but you never interact with any of these people anymore."

"What do you mean, Reverend?"

"Toni, you've become disconnected from the living in the results of your service. It seems now your only connection is what you do for the dead. You were able to deal with the things you experienced in Vietnam by focusing on your service there, on its results and by focusing on others. Many times you've told me the stories of the relatives of the soldiers and how much it meant to them that you had been there when their loved ones died."

"I know."

"With this work you do, I think you've found a way lately to anesthetize yourself from that a little."

"I see what you mean," I said. It was hard to hear, but I realized that what he said was true. It was easier to deal with the pain of what I had seen and done in Vietnam and in my work here by distancing myself from it.

"Now it's hitting close to home again with Teddy," Reverend Iordani continued. "It's hitting close to home and your thoughts are about what it will mean to you and what you will go through. Focus needs to be redirected to Irini, Gregory and Eleni, and what it will mean to them to finally have this resolved. Your service to others is the focus—away from yourself and to the needs of those you serve. It is only through selflessness that we can heal our internal pain."

"Yes," I said, looking down at the crushed granite on the trail. I pushed some of it around with the toe of my boot. Easier to say and to understand than to do.

He placed his hand gently on mine.

"I want you to go with me this afternoon. I have a visit to make to a local seniors' home. I want you to meet some people."

Maria Pappas was seventy-eight and her husband, George, was eighty-two. They were both small, frail people. Maria was only about five-one and George was maybe five-four, tops. They both had thick, dark, coarse hair peppered lightly with gray. George didn't know anybody anymore and couldn't do anything for himself. He lived at Riverview Assisted Living. Maria lived there with him and waited on him hand and foot. She had to do everything for him.

Their little apartment was very nicely decorated. It consisted of a sitting room and a kitchenette with a small table and two chairs, a bedroom and a bath. It was small, but Maria had made it warm and cozy with her furniture. Many beautiful pictures hung on the walls around us. An old and well-used Bible rested on a table near the door.

Reverend Iordani said some special prayers and then we all sat down in the sitting room to visit. Unhampered by the kitchenette's limited resources, Maria had made us a wonderful snack of koulouria—Greek butter cookies—served us Greek coffee, took care of all of George's needs, and all of ours. I tried to help her, as did Reverend Iordani, but she wouldn't have it. At seventy-eight, she had more energy then I did thirty years ago.

She spoke of the past, the good times with George. Her hands trembled when she lifted the coffee cup. She spent the entire visit reminiscing about those days. If George made a sound or moved, she attended to him immediately. I saw then that there was fatigue there, too, but she would not and could not give up. Something inside her gave her that energy—the energy to continue. Her energy came from love—selfless love.

Reverend Iordani was right. I had become disconnected. In turning too inward, I had become selfish with my service. Suddenly it occurred to me—watching Maria tend to George and listening to her talk about their old days together—I thought about Irini trapped in those days of Vietnam all this time, never able to fully move on. To move on would be to leave Teddy there, and she could never leave Teddy alone, any more than Maria Pappas would leave George. This wasn't just about freeing Ted, it was about freeing Irini—and Irini could never be free until Ted came home where she knew he would be safe forever.

❧ Chapter Six ❧

I had laid down the initial layer of clay on the Red Bud victim and had stepped back to check it all over. I would leave for Hawaii in less than a week. I wanted to get this sculpture completed before I left, so photos of the face could be disseminated on television and in the papers, and a possible ID made while I was gone.

The face was round, with broad cheeks that had a slight flatness to them. The nose was short, narrow at the bridge and then flaring to become much wider toward the end. Her brow line was straight from the nose bridge, only arching slightly over the eyes. Her rounded face circled the broad cheeks to a soft, small chin. It wasn't a glamorous or particularly remarkable face, but it was a sweet one. I was getting to know her and beginning to feel an even greater sorrow at thinking how this lovely woman could have been killed and dumped this way.

I was now at the stage where the intuitive part of my work would begin. The science of tissue depths had been applied to all areas of the face. Normally, I would take into account clothing found with the victim and any other personal articles to give me an impression of the person as I finalized the face, but in this case, there was nothing but a jumble of bones in a makeshift grave, and one sad scrap of flowered cloth.

I thought about what Leo had said about the grave site and the method of death, and about the kind of killing she thought it was. This woman's identity would tell us a lot about her life, with whom she might have been involved, or who she would have encountered that could have done this to her. Who was she and where had she been buried for those years before she turned up on the river's edge at Red Bud Isle? Were it not for an early-morning kayaker, her bones would have washed down the Colorado River in anonymity.

I sat on the stool in front of my workbench just looking at the bust as it was. I sat there in my blue-jean cutoffs and an old, faded red T-shirt, with my bare feet propped up on the rungs of the stool. I let the image of the face as it was permeate my thoughts until I felt that I could "see" the person as she had been—until I could feel something of who she was.

When I look at faces I see shapes and the way those shapes come together to form the image of that person. Most eyewitnesses' identifications of criminals are faulty, not only because of suggestions that might have been made, but mostly because of the way most people observe other people. They "snapshot" the view and then they do something that totally distorts the memory—they make a judgment about what they saw. They form an opinion.

I decided, based on my years of experience with faces, how I thought her eyes and nose should look—on the aspect of her expression. I had to breathe some artistic life into the static clay reconstruct. I would work through the night to finish this one. I would have to add more clay to smooth the features of the face across the tissue-depth markers, without adding any depth that would distort the image. At the same time, some knowledge and experience would come into play to interpret what had been there before she died. It would be early morning before I was through with all that, but there would be time to catch up on sleep on the way to Hawaii next week. Meanwhile, there was hard work to be done and a lost woman to be found.

Drew Smith had called and asked if he could come by. There was a development in our Cottonwood case. I told him to come on over, and I went into the kitchen to put on a pot of tea. I checked the cookie jar and discovered that my son had managed to actually leave some of my sugar cookies there. There were enough for Drew and me to share while we drank our tea. I decided to brew a really good green tea with jasmine. It was one I had discovered recently and I thought Drew might like it. He was a real tea drinker, and it was difficult for me to find something original for him to drink.

While the water heated to a boil, I went into the other room to put on something more decent than cutoffs and a faded old T-shirt. I changed into a pair of good jeans and a black round-neck knit top.

The whistle on the teapot began to go off just as the doorbell rang. I turned down the fire on the stove and went to the door. Drew stood on my front porch in jeans and a red golf shirt with a blue windbreaker over it, and a manila file in his hand.

"Casual attire?" I said.

"Officially off duty today."

"Oh. So, of course you're working on your day off."

"Contrary to popular titles, death does not take any holidays."

I smiled and motioned for him to come in. He looked toward the kitchen and sniffed thoughtfully, a question in his brow.

"Green tea with jasmine," I said.

He smiled. "Now, that's a new one for me."

Yes! I thought. Out loud I said, "*And* my home-made sugar cookies."

Drew shook his head and smiled. "Now, Toni, you are going to just spoil me."

"It gets better," I said. "It's your mama's recipe for the cookies."

"Oh no. I hope you don't have very many of them, because I have just managed to take off five pounds I gained from slacking off at the gym last month. I had to work out double time for two solid weeks. If you've got Mama's sugar cookies, I could regain the whole five pounds in one sitting." And then he laughed.

Now I shook my head. "Well, lucky for you, my son was over here the other day and he polished off quite a few of them before I managed to run him off."

"Thank goodness," he chuckled. "All the time at the gym will not be wasted now."

He smiled that great smile with his gentle overbite. Drew had married when he was twenty-one and divorced before he was twenty-seven. His wife had left him for someone else. Drew said it was because she couldn't handle his police work—he had been a state trooper then. Still, I wondered what that crazy woman must have been thinking. Drew was a treasure. I hated to be a matchmaker, but I just knew there must be a nice young woman out there for him somewhere.

I plated the cookies and poured our tea. Drew laid the file on the table and took off his windbreaker, hung it on the back of his chair and waited. He would never sit down until all the ladies in the room were seated. I sat and then he sat. I made a mental note to look much harder to find a nice girl for him. He would have been embarrassed to know that, but he would never know. I could be sneaky when I wanted to be.

We chatted for a while. He asked how Michael was and I asked about his mother. Mama Beatrice was doing well, he told me, but she was thinking about leaving Louisiana and moving to Austin to be closer to Drew. She was getting up in years and thought that living closer to her son would be wise. Drew's sister lived in San Antonio and both of his brothers worked in Houston. Mama Beatrice didn't like either of those places as well as Austin. Plus, I knew that Drew was the one of her children who took care of things for her.

I told Drew I'd be happy to help her find a place and relocate. I would love to have my friend Beatrice in the city. Drew said he'd take me up on that, and he'd keep me posted on her plans.

"So, what is new on our cottonwood case that has caused you to work on your day off?"

"She's been identified."

I set my teacup down. This was always the moment for which I worked and waited.

"Her name is Lisa Wells."

I sat still for a moment. This young girl with whom I had become so connected and whose face had come to life again under my fingertips—this young girl was reconnected with her name and her history.

"How did you find out who she was?"

"Her mother saw the photos of the bust on the local TV news and recognized her. She called the number on the screen, and wanted to come in and identify her daughter."

I sighed a deep sigh. "Oh man."

"Yeah. I had to explain to her as gently as I could that it would not be possible. Then I explained that I would need her daughter's dental records and we would confirm the ID."

"How did she take it when you explained?"

"Pretty hard. I cushioned the news as much as I could, but there aren't a lot of sweet ways you can tell a mother that her daughter's remains consist of bones that lay exposed in a cottonwood grove for months and have been picked clean by buzzards."

I ran my hand through my hair and sighed again.

"Sorry, Toni."

"No, it's not what you said. I deal with that truth on almost every case I have. It's...just thinking about that mother."

"Yeah."

"Where was the victim from?"

"She lived in Dallas with her boyfriend, but the mother, Gladys, lives in Athens, just east of Dallas."

"So, do we have any clue who killed Lisa Wells?"

"We do. Her mother says she was living with a man named Johnathan Rowell. The police had been called to their home numerous times for domestic violence. Lisa had been hospitalized several times for broken bones. Each time, she went back to him and charges were dropped."

"Great. So, has he been charged yet?"

"Now wait."

I sighed.

"Let me finish. We collected as much evidence as we could from the crime scene. The body had been wrapped in a blanket, and we checked that against fibers we took from the trunk of Rowell's car."

"That's a long shot. Plus, if the blanket belonged to them, why *wouldn't* fibers from it be in the car?"

"The blanket didn't belong to them." Drew smiled.

"Give," I said, shooting him a look.

"I showed the blanket to Mrs. Wells when she came down to claim the remains. She said she didn't recognize that particular blanket, but that it looked similar to something that Rita's mother had made."

"And Rita is...?"

"Lisa's best friend. Her mother handweaves blankets, rugs, you get the picture."

"So..."

"So, I contacted Rita—Rita Gallekamp—Rita says the blanket was hers. It was new and her mom had made it for her. She brought it over to Lisa's the night before Lisa disappeared. Rita's husband was out of town, and Johnny was out playing cards and drinking with his friends, and Rita and Lisa had decided to watch a movie on TV, eat popcorn, and have some fun—you know, a girls' night in. Rita gets cold easily and she brought the blanket because she said Lisa's place was always cold. Johnny kept the apartment cold, and he'd get mad if Lisa turned the heat up."

"Cheap?"

"Yep."

"So, the place was always cold and she brought her blanket."

"She also wanted to show it to Lisa because it was new and her mom had just made it for her and given it to her as a birthday gift."

"So, how did it wind up wrapped around Lisa's discarded body?"

"Rita left the blanket there by accident. She was going to go back and get it the next day, but then Lisa disappeared. She asked Johnny to look for it, but it was gone. Johnny told Rita that maybe Lisa had taken it with her. Rita's mother was real mad about the blanket. Rita kept thinking that Lisa would call her, but they never heard from her, and Rita never got the blanket back."

"Any chance Rita was involved in this?"

"Not in my book. Rita is happily married, and she was Lisa's best friend since they were eight. According to Lisa's mother, Rita couldn't stand Johnny, and she had begged Lisa to leave him a million times. She still hates him. Also, she and her husband have since moved to San Antonio—the husband got transferred."

"Hmm. Interesting. Still, the fiber is a long shot."

Drew smiled. "We also have Johnny's credit records for the time period when Lisa would have been dumped in that cottonwood grove. Hutto is a long ways from Dallas."

"So, you're looking for any receipts that tie him to the area near Hutto."

"Bingo. Lisa's mother said that to her knowledge they did not make any trips anywhere within three months before Lisa disappeared. Lisa and Johnny didn't have much money, and he spent what they did have on drinking and playing cards with his friends."

"So, you might have a chance if you can tie him to this area."

"Right. Also, that handmade blanket was real different."

"What do you mean?"

"State Crime Lab says the fibers are very unique, so a match would be a good, solid match."

"Drew, he's probably cleaned that car a million times since then."

"We only need one fiber match to nail the creep."

I nodded. "I sure hope that one fiber is there."

"That's not all I have up my sleeve, Toni."

"What else?"

"We Luminoled that car—the trunk, the back seat, the carpets—all of it."

Luminol was a chemical the police used to spray on suspicious areas in a crime scene, or somewhere they suspected bore a relationship to a crime—like a suspect's car. Luminol attached itself to blood proteins, and when illuminated by the right kind of light, it fluoresced to reveal those blood proteins. That stuff would show blood proteins on a wall where the blood had been scrubbed and painted over with latex paint. It was a great forensic tool.

"So, you found something with the Luminol?"

Drew nodded. "There were some spots in the trunk, and we took samples. The lab analyzed all of it."

"I hope it's her blood."

"Meanwhile, I didn't give up on his credit card records."

Drew had patience, too. He would never push a case to the D.A. until he thought he had it airtight. Early in his career, a young and overzealous Drew Smith had made that mistake and the killer had gotten off, never to be tried again. Drew had never forgotten the sting of double jeopardy, and he carried that sting into the diligence he brought to each case he handled.

So we knew her name was Lisa Wells. We knew who her mother was and how long Lisa had been missing. We knew where she had lived and with whom. We knew who we thought had killed her. We had gone from being completely mystified about the death of an anonymous woman whose remains were found in a grove of cottonwood trees, to knowing all these things about her—and we had made that jump to light-speed by televising a picture of the bust I had made from her skull. These were the kind of results I dreamed of on every case I worked.

"You found something in the credit card records."

"Well, Toni, let's not get ahead of my story." He smiled mischievously and sipped his tea.

"So tell me," I said.

He opened the file that had been sitting there all this time, then pulled out two photographs and handed one of them to me.

"You see this," he said. "This is a microscopic photo of a fiber taken from the blanket we found wrapped around Lisa Wells's remains."

"Okay."

"It's a very distinctive fiber, I'm told."

"So I heard."

He smiled again and handed me the second photograph.

"This fiber is the same kind of photo of a fiber we took from the trunk of Johnny Rowell's car."

"They look similar to me and I'm not a fiber expert."

"I'm told by someone who *is* a fiber expert that they are dead-bang duplicates of each other. In other words, they came from the same blanket."

"Awesome!"

He chuckled with satisfaction.

"I'm not done yet."

"What have you got now?"

"You know the Luminol?

"Yes..."

"You know the blood-protein spots we found?"

"Yes..."

"We found some spatters near the same spare-tire compartment, which is where we also found the fiber. It's human blood, Lisa Wells's blood type, and we're testing it for DNA."

"You got samples of her DNA from her bones."

"Yep, it was still viable. It'll be a while before we get the DNA back, but meanwhile we know it was human blood, and it was her type."

"You've got all your bases covered, don't you, Drew."

"I try, Toni."

"It's all really good when you combine it with the fiber evidence."

"I have one more trick up my sleeve."

"You're kidding."

"I told you I didn't give up on those credit card receipts."

He handed me a photocopy. On the page was a copy of a gas card receipt.

"It's from his credit card, and as you can see, the address of the truck stop on the receipt is..."

"Hutto, Texas."

"Yeahhhh." He grinned and nodded his head in total satisfaction.

"He was actually stupid enough to fill up in Hutto before he left?"

"Well, you've never met Johnny Rowell, Toni, but...well, let's just say he's not exactly the sharpest knife in the drawer."

We both laughed out loud now.

"This is rich, Drew—just totally, completely rich."

"Oh yeah. He's been arrested for beating her multiple times and she dropped the charges every time. There's no one to drop charges now other than the prosecutor, and she won't be dropping anything. This guy is finally going down."

"I just wish the system had stopped him before Lisa Wells had to die."

"So do I, Toni, but you and I cannot overhaul the system overnight. What we can do is what we did. I picked up Johnny Rowell in Dallas yesterday and he is now in jail without bail."

"You're amazing, Drew."

"No, Toni, it's just good persistent police work, that's all. It wasn't just me anyway. It was you and your awesome artwork, and the people in the State Crime Lab hustling to get me that fiber and blood evidence."

Now I waited on similar results from the bust I had made of the skull found on Red Bud Isle. I decided to tell Drew about that case.

"I'm glad we were able to close this one," I said. "I hope we can achieve the same results on the case I'm currently working on."

"Are these your bones found on the riverbank the other morning?"

I nodded. "Get this, Drew. A complete skeleton just dumped in a shallow grave on the dam side of Red Bud Isle. Bones were not in anatomical order—they were just dumped in a jumble in this grave."

"So the bones were dumped there after the body decomposed?"

"The 'body' had been buried somewhere else before. There was soil of a different type in the crevices of some of the bones. Chris has sent the various soil samples off to A&M for analysis."

"The deceased had been buried before...."

"Yes. What do you think about that?"

"I think it's different for sure. I've never heard of anything like that. Any idea what's going on there?"

I told him about Leo's impression of the murder. He sat and listened intently as I repeated what Leo had told me the day before.

He nodded. "Now that you explain everything the way she said it, I can see what she means. I actually remember a case where a man killed his neighbor and the neighbor's wife because he thought they were vandalizing his treasured gardens."

"You can't be serious."

"Oh yes, totally. The guy was a kind of weird guy, didn't really get along with anybody, wasn't really good at anything except gardening. He spent all his time on his yard. I have to admit it did look good. He never socialized with his neighbors and he and the victims had apparently gotten off to a bad start when he moved in because of something stupid that he said. It seems from that day forward he imagined that they were out to get him."

"Were they really vandalizing his gardens?"

"No. Actually there was a rash of some of that going on in the neighborhood and it turned out to be nothing more than some smart-aleck high-school kids looking for something to do at night. But this guy was sure the culprits were his next-door neighbors."

"So, what happened?"

"One day he came home from work and saw that his prized magnolia tree had been cut down right in the front yard and he just went nuts. He went in the house, got his shotgun, marched right through the back door of his neighbor's house and shot him and his wife eating dinner at the kitchen table."

"Good grief!"

"It was the most unbelievable thing I'd ever seen. Just shot 'em at nearly point-blank range—bang, bang, and that was it. He tried to run, but I pulled him over about forty miles out of town. He shot at me, and I managed to just wing him. He's still serving time in Huntsville."

"That's incredible. Killed two people over a magnolia tree."

"A magnolia tree they had nothing to do with."

"I can't even absorb that."

"There are a lot of real wackos out there, Toni. He was just totally paranoid, but he was real cool about killing them. Said he had thought about it a lot. He had planned what he would do, he just waited to do it until something set him off."

"That sounds like the kind of thing Leo was talking about."

"I'd like you to keep me up to date on this. If it turns out the original burial site is outside of Austin, that's something I'd want to know."

I nodded and agreed to keep him apprised.

Chapter Seven

Jimmy Hughes saw the round face with the broad cheeks, small chin and full lips on the screen of his television on the six-o'clock local news. It was a ghost—the face of a woman missing for sixteen years, a girl from his hometown, a girl from Viola, a girl he had loved since he was eighteen. Her name had been Adelaide Russell—"Addie" they called her. She was only fourteen then, and he was off to Vietnam. Addie may have been fourteen, but Jimmy had known her all of her fourteen years, and he loved her. At eighteen, Jimmy was still a boy in his heart and Addie was a pretty young girl with long, blond hair. Jimmy went to Vietnam and came back and Addie was dating someone else. Later, she married, had two children, and then disappeared at the age of thirty-two. That was sixteen years ago.

Jimmy had called the number on the screen and spoken to Tommy Lucero. Tommy had asked him to come in.

"So, what was he like?" I asked as I put lunch on the table.

Tommy shrugged. "You know, typical overage-hippie type. The normal Austin citizen."

"I don't know, Tommy," Mike chimed in. "I think the guy looked like he'd tried to dress up, sort of. He was wearing dark green cords and a real clean T-shirt. I think he had even pressed the shirt a little."

"The cords were old, man."

"Yeah, but they were clean—and they looked pressed, too." He looked at me. "It wasn't one of your ironing jobs, Mario, but it wasn't bad for a bachelor."

Tommy smiled at the use of my nickname. He made a grab for the fresh bread, and I slapped his hand gently.

"Hey, dude, we say grace first in this house," Mike said.

"You're one to talk, young man, since you're notorious for grabbing food first and saying grace later," I admonished.

Tommy chuckled.

"So, then I'll offer the grace," Mike said.

I sat down at the table with them, and Mike did offer the grace. Then the two men tore into that food like two hungry wolves. You'd think they were sixteen-year-olds still growing two inches every six months.

"So, he made an attempt to look good," I said, "but not for either one of you characters. Could he have wanted to look good for her?"

Mike nodded. "I think so." He slugged down almost his entire glass of tea in one gulp.

"What are you talking about?" Tommy said. "She's dead and he knew that—he ID'd the face from the news."

"Tommy, I'm telling you, that guy thought he was going to identify a body."

"No. I totally disagree. She's been dead sixteen years. We had to have her face reconstructed. No one in their right mind would think he was going to ID a body."

"Okay, man—whatever."

I could tell this had been a running argument all day. I poured both of them some more tea. Tommy grabbed a fresh lemon wedge, squeezed it into his tea and then dropped the wedge into the glass.

"So, what else did this guy tell you?"

"She's some girl from his hometown," Tommy said. "He had some kind of crush on her or something. When she disappeared, she was married to a guy named Dody Waldrep. We checked the records in Viola and there is no Dody Waldrep there anymore, but we found the woman's mother, Maureen Russell. She still lives there."

"Yeah, she says that Dody lives in Manor now. They don't keep in touch. She raised Addie's two children for the last fourteen years—two girls— twenty-two and twenty-four now."

"So, what was the story with the dad? Why did Grandma get the kids?"

"Dad drinks, ever since Mom skipped," Tommy said.

"Skipped?"

"Mrs. Russell said we would hear all the rumors anyway, so she would just tell us. She says the townspeople thought that her daughter was having an affair, and that she ran off with the man. She disappeared sixteen years ago, and so did he."

"So, Mom—ask who he was."

"This Jimmy Hughes who identified her?"

"Anhh, you lose twenty-five thousand dollars and the trip to Bermuda," Mike said.

"Okay, smarty, who was it?"

"Jimmy's brother, Doug," Tommy said, nodding.

"Interesting."

We all ate in silence awhile. I watched while the food evaporated from the table.

"So, what did this Jimmy say about his brother's disappearance?"

"We didn't know all that when we interviewed him this morning, so we haven't had a chance to ask him."

"Yeah, Mario, you're getting ahead of us again. We just talked to Mrs. Russell on the phone a little while ago. There hasn't been time for us to go up to Viola and see her in person, or to find and talk to Dody Waldrep, the victim's husband, much less go back and question Jimmy again."

"But Jimmy must have said something this morning about his brother's disappearance—right?"

The two men looked at each other and then at me, and shook their heads in unison.

"Weird, huh, Toni?"

"To say the least. So, he just came in and identified the woman and told you who she was and a little bit about how he knew her, and that was it?"

"Yep," Mike said as he dabbed up the last bit of food from his plate with a piece of bread.

"We couldn't get anything else out of him. He was quiet and kind of edgylike, but he was almost belligerent in his answers a few times."

"I agree with that," Mike said. "He wasn't trying to cooperate, really. I mean, he identified her by calling in, and then coming in to talk, but he wasn't forthcoming after he got there."

"No sign of grief?"

"That's hard to say, Toni. It was hard to tell what was going on with this guy. He was kind of withdrawn sometimes, and then like I said, he'd be belligerent. He was a tough read—strange, and a really tough read."

"I'd like to go talk to him, if you don't mind. You know, when people find out that I'm the one who sculpted their friend's or family member's face, they sometimes open up."

Mike sighed. My son had issues with me "interfering" in his cases, but I had issues with leaving my sculptures alone—both before and after they reacquired their identities. I had already become involved with Addie Russell Waldrep before I knew that's who she was. I had held her skull. I knew every square millimeter of her face. She and I had made a connection across the expanse of time—we had a kind of spiritual friendship. I wanted to help find who killed her. I *had* to find who killed her.

"I don't mind," Tommy said, "for the usual deal."

"I tell you everything I find out."

"Yep—and we're still going to see him again later anyway, whether you go or not. It's our job, you know."

"I understand, Tommy. You know I understand."

He nodded. "Go talk to him, then. I'll give you the phone number and address."

Mike sighed again, and Tommy shook his head and smiled.

"Hey, Toni, take Leo with you—Okay?"

"Not in her uniform. He won't talk to me."

"I didn't say she had to be in uniform. Just take her, and tell her I said to wear that ankle holster I gave her."

I sighed, "Right."

"Tommy's rules, Mario."

"I heard, son."

* * *

My Black Beauty rumbled to a stop in front of a dinky frame house in one of the old Central/West Austin neighborhoods. There were rows of small one-story houses on narrow little lots. Built in the late 1940s and early 1950s for the postwar set, it was affordable middle-class housing for mostly blue-collar folk...pretty stylish then, but out-of-date now and way overpriced. The houses were pretty light-weight stuff compared to the new construction in Austin, but people lived in these neighborhoods for the convenience and the atmosphere of Central/West Austin.

Jimmy's house was chartreuse with brown and magenta trim and a tin roof—and that was the re-furbished look. The yard was marginal—a combination of Bermuda grass and weeds with patches of hard, dry dirt. The shrubs that went across the front of the house were patchy—one green and looking fairly healthy, but shaggy, next to another that looked more like tumbleweed. There was a gravel driveway that led to the carport, where his 1968 Ford pickup truck was parked. It was dark green, with patches of primer and brown paint. There was a bumper sticker on the back with the symbol of the POWs/MIAs and the slogan Lest We Forget, and the back windshield bore the emblem of the United States Marines, next to which was another bumper sticker that simply read, Semper Fi.

"Interesting color scheme," Leo said.

"At least the door is brown," I said as I knocked on the door frame.

Jimmy Hughes came to the door wearing an undershirt and faded, torn blue jeans—there were no shoes on his feet. A chocolate-brown Lab stood by his side. He stared at us from behind the screen door. He was about six feet tall, slim, with a narrow face and square chin. He had piercing light blue eyes and long dark eyelashes. His gray hair was thin on top with a receding hairline, but it was long in back and pulled into a ponytail held by a green rubber band. The most noticeable thing about Jimmy's appearance was a long scar that ran down the left cheek, and burn wounds on either cheek and near his left eye.

"Jimmy Hughes?"

"Yeah," he said suspiciously.

"My name is Toni, and I'm the artist who sculpted the face of Addie Russell that you saw on the news."

"Oh yeah?" His face brightened just a bit.

"Would you mind if we came in and talked just awhile? I'd like to know more about her."

He looked at Leo and squinted.

"This is my friend, Leo."

"Y'all work for the cops?"

"No," I said.

It was true. Neither Leo nor I were employed by the police. I was a freelance artist who contracted with anyone who requested my services, and Leo was employed by the AFD, although technically she was a law enforcement officer. He looked us both over carefully and then motioned us in.

"It ain't fancy, nor even neat," he said as we entered.

There were books and magazines scattered about on the floor and on any even surface in the room—coffee table, end table, bookshelf—you name it. An old recliner sat on one end of the living room, right across from a small TV. The recliner was upholstered in a tacky plaid and it had a large hole in the fabric on one arm. There was a guitar leaning up against the wall next to the recliner. Jimmy motioned us to the sofa, which was also worn, but was one of the only places in the room not covered with books and magazines.

Nodding toward the guitar I said, "You play?"

"Yes ma'am," he said, "I play a couple of gigs a week with some guys. We play rhythm and blues."

"My husband and I used to listen to that kind of music. There was a man in my husband's unit in Vietnam who used to play guitar for us in the evenings. That is, when we weren't on duty or under mortar fire."

He turned his head and leaned toward me on the edge of his chair. "You were in 'Nam?"

I nodded. "U.S. Air Force. I was a nurse in Da Nang. My husband and I met over there."

He relaxed almost instantly.

"I was in the marines. I was in Da Nang for a while, too."

"We had a lot of friends who were marines," I said. "When were you there?"

"I was 'in country' 1968 to 1970. I was in Da Nang toward the end of 1968 and some of 1969."

"We were already gone by then," I said.

He nodded. We sat quietly for a few seconds.

"Is that how you make your living, Jimmy—playing the guitar?"

"Well, it's one way. I do some writing for the *Freedom Journal*."

"Yes, I've heard of that paper."

It was a strange paper that had an occasional good article, but most of their pieces were pretty much all over the map.

"It doesn't pay much, but I get a little bit per article. Then I also work down at the canoe and paddleboat rental place on Barton Creek."

"I know that place," Leo said. "So, are you a boater yourself?"

"I like to go out on the water, paddle up and down Town Lake and just think sometimes. It's quiet out there and sometimes I just need that kind of quiet."

"I can relate to that," I said.

I looked at Leo and caught her eye. Leo and I looked at each other, and I knew she was thinking what I was about the canoeing. Then I glanced down and saw a pair of hiking boots on the floor near his chair. They had red clay caked up all around the soles. I recognized that thick red clay—it was the same red clay I had on my boots from Red Bud Isle that morning we dug up Addie Waldrep's bones. It could be a coincidence, but I still wondered about it.

"So, Jimmy, would you mind telling me about Addie—how you knew her?"

"What's your interest?"

"I reconstructed her face and I guess I got a little attached to her."

The expression on his face was strange in response to my words—I couldn't tell if it was sorrow or nervousness. He cleared his throat and shifted in his seat. "Well, uh, we grew up together in this little-bitty town. You probably never heard of it—Viola?"

"Actually, I have heard of it. It's up near Giddings, right?"

"Uh, yeah, that's right. Well, Addie was about four years younger than me, but I knew her since she was born. Her family lived just down the road from mine, and we went to the same school."

"Was she an only child?"

"No. She had a brother. I think he lives in Houston now."

"Do you have any brothers or sisters?"

"My baby brother, Vernon, lives in Rock Hill right near Viola. Mama lives there now, too. My other little brother, Doug, moved there first, then Vernon and Mama did, too."

"You don't live there anymore."

"When I got back from 'Nam, I couldn't live there anymore. Everything was different. I didn't like it. I moved here. I like it here."

I nodded. He fidgeted with his hands, and shifted in his chair a lot. His mood seemed to swing from being more at ease to eyeing us suspiciously. I tried to keep my questions in the "innocent" category, to draw him out and see if he would volunteer anything to me.

"So, you knew Addie in Viola growing up, but your family moved to Rock Hill. When did your family move?"

"Not long after I got back from 'Nam, my daddy died and I moved here. Doug bought a place down at Rock Hill, and that's when they all moved. It's nice, I guess. Vernon runs Doug's place now."

That was the opening I was waiting for.

"Where is Doug?"

He looked nervous, and started to look angry. He glanced down at the floor and his aspect changed, and he looked up and said, "Doug went missing about the time Addie did."

I acted surprised. "Oh." I waited in silence, but my gaze never left him.

He sighed. "Rumor was that he and Addie had something going. Then they disappeared at exactly the same time."

"What do you think—was he involved with Addie?"

He became more agitated. "No way."

"How do you know?"

"Just do, that's all."

"You've never heard from Doug?"

"No."

"Didn't you think that was strange?"

"Well, of course I thought it was strange," he snapped. "But what was I going to do about it?"

He leaned back in the chair now. He crossed his right foot over on top of his left leg. He was about to shut down on me, and I didn't want that to happen. I wanted to know what he was withholding.

"I'm sorry, Jimmy, I didn't mean it to sound that way. I guess I was just surprised that you hadn't heard from him."

He sat forward in the chair and rubbed his hands together while looking down at his feet.

"It just upsets me is all."

He shrugged. I wanted to ask him all my questions, get the answers and leave, but he would never give up the information that way. I had to play my game, and go slowly. It was nerve-wracking. I looked over at Leo, who had been watching him carefully the whole time. She nodded slightly as if to confirm that I should continue.

"Tell me more about Addie, Jimmy."

He lightened up a little, and then said, "Well, she was real pretty when we were kids. I had a crush on her, but she was fourteen, so I knew I had to wait till she was old enough to date. I got called to 'Nam, so I enlisted with the marines. I went off to 'Nam and she was all I thought about. I dreamed about being able to come back home and see Addie."

"What happened?"

"When I got home she was already dating a guy named Dody Waldrep. I thought they'd break up. I didn't think he was right for her. I figured she'd figure that out, but she stuck with him. He never did deserve her."

I wondered if Jimmy thought anyone deserved Addie Russell Waldrep.

"Is that why you're so sure she wasn't involved with your brother?"

He knitted his forehead and rubbed his hands together harder.

"I told you, I just know, that's all." He got up out of his chair. "Listen, I don't feel like talking anymore. I got things to do before my gig tonight."

We were being shuttled out. I hadn't learned as much as I wanted, but I had learned what Jimmy Hughes didn't want to talk about, and what he didn't want to say might prove to be more interesting than anything he had said.

✑ Chapter Eight ✑

My son and his partner attended a lot of funerals. Serial killings get a lot of attention in the news, but the vast majority of killings are personal in nature, committed by someone the victim knew. Because of that, it's likely that the murderer might show up at the funeral, or that someone's absence from the funeral, or actions at the funeral, might be of note. Mike and Tommy routinely attended the funerals of the victims in their cases just so they could observe all the people who were and were not there. Such was the case with the funeral of Addie Waldrep.

Addie Waldrep had been missing for sixteen years. It was assumed that she had run off with Doug Hughes, who was thought to be her lover and who had also been missing for sixteen years. No one had ever heard from either one of them again. Now the question on all of our minds was who had killed her, and whether Doug himself had become a victim also. The list of suspects was just beginning to be developed, and at least for now even the missing Doug Hughes was on the list.

At the time of Addie's disappearance, she and her husband, Dody, and their two daughters had been living in Viola, which is about an hour southeast of Austin. It was a small spot on one of those farm-to-market roads off of Highway 290. Viola was their hometown.

There had been rumors about Addie's relationship with Doug. Doug had lived in Rock Hill just as Jimmy had told us. Doug ran what became his family's farm. His father had died, Doug had bought the farm in Rock Hill, and he and his brother Vernon worked the farm together. His mother still lived there, and Vernon and his wife and family lived there, too.

One day Doug and Addie had simply disappeared. Now Addie had been found. No one had seen or heard from Doug since he disappeared with Addie.

Still, rumors or no, Maureen Russell and Doug's mother, Gloria Hughes, never believed that their children were either having an affair or had run off together. Maureen made it clear to Mike and Tommy that she considered Dody Waldrep to be the prime suspect in the death of her daughter. The question was whether she based that on any real suspicion, or just on the fact that she despised Dody—and she made no bones about the fact that she did despise him.

Gloria Hughes had told Mike and Tommy that Doug had a girlfriend—a young girl named Lori Webster. Lori lived in Georgetown now, and the boys had gone to speak to her before the funeral, but I had not had time to get the details of that interview.

Addie's funeral was in the nearby town of Giddings—a metropolis compared to Viola and Rock Hill. The burial would be in a little community cemetery in Viola where Addie's two daughters lived with Maureen Russell. It seemed that Dody had a drinking problem. So the girls had gone to live with their grandmother. Dody had moved to Manor, got himself a house out on an acre of land and a job in Austin working for a plumbing company. The girls rarely saw him. They didn't even remember their mother.

Standing in the funeral home next to my son and Tommy, I could see down the aisle to the family section. The two girls sat looking sad and confused next to Mrs. Russell. Mrs. Russell wept unceasingly for her daughter, wiping her eyes and nose. It seemed that everyone in the town was there, and after paying respects to Addie, each person filed past her mother and two children and gave their condolences. Mike informed me that Lori Webster was not there.

I smelled him before I saw him. The rank smell of nicotine was the first attack on my olfactory senses. Then the too-sweet smell of last night's bourbon joined the wave of putrid odors that washed my way as he passed down the aisle. I looked to my right to see who this was as he passed by.

Michael nudged me slightly with his elbow. "Dody Waldrep," he whispered.

I nodded.

In his wake, new odors assaulted me—now, the stale smell of unwashed hair mixed with the sourness of sweat. Dody looked about ten or fifteen years older than Mike had told me he was. He was thin and his skin was weathered and flushed from an obvious alcohol habit. He wore khaki workman's trousers over his skinny legs, and a worn plaid shirt was stretched over his protruding beer gut and tucked into the waistband of his pants. Except for the gut, Dody Waldrep was so thin and frail, that I imagine he'd have weighed a hundred forty pounds soaking wet. His thin, greasy hair was combed straight back from his ruddy face.

Dody didn't appear terribly grief stricken, but considering that his wife had allegedly left him for someone else over sixteen years ago, grief isn't what I would have expected. He had completely let himself go and he had abdicated the care of his children to his mother-in-law, but there was a kind of pathetic aspect to him, and I felt sorry for him in a way. I was surprised he showed up. He had the shakes and he was sweating. He didn't look well, but then, a lot of alcoholics don't look well, especially when they're sober. It looked as though Dody Waldrep had sobered up for this. He started to sit with his daughters, but one look from his mother-in-law said it all, and he sat down in the row behind them.

I watched him throughout the service. He didn't weep, but he looked upset. Mostly he just looked terribly depressed and beaten. I think for Dody it had been another reliving of an old shame. I wondered if a man who looked that lost could have committed such a crime. It was hard to tell just by watching him there. One thing I had learned for sure in all my years was not to jump to any conclusions until all the facts were in, or at least more facts than we currently had in this case.

Dody didn't attend the graveside services. In fact, he disappeared in the crowd right after the funeral. At the cemetery, I noticed a woman weeping softly, and then talking for some time with Addie's mother. I leaned over toward my son.

"Who's the woman in navy talking to Addie's mother?"

"That is Gloria Hughes, Doug Hughes's mother." He raised his eyebrows.

I returned the raised eyebrows with, "Really."

Mike nodded. "She says she's heard nothing from Doug in all these years. The brother, Vernon, confirms that."

"That's what Jimmy says also. What do you think?"

Mike shrugged. "I don't know, Mom. I guess I believe Vernon and Mrs. Hughes, but Jimmy is odd. I'm not sure what's up with him."

I nodded in agreement. I couldn't decide if he had problems from the war or if it was something else.

"Mrs. Hughes got real upset and asked us what we thought the chances were that Doug might still be alive."

"What'd you tell her?"

"The truth. That I don't have any idea. That I have no evidence that Addie's murder is connected to Doug and that I don't know any more about it than that."

The truth was, the thought that Doug might also be dead had occurred to us all. The alternative to that was that Doug had killed Addie. There was some outside chance that he and Addie had split up and that Addie's fate had been completely unknown to him. If that were true, though, we all felt that Doug would have contacted his mother years ago. The fact that no one had ever heard from him again led us all to believe that he had either been killed with Addie, or had done the killing. I personally considered the former to be a better bet.

"Did you question Dody Waldrep yet?"

"Oh yeah," Mike responded.

"So, what was your impression?"

"I don't like him," Tommy replied.

"That's succinct," I said.

"Aside from smelling really bad and being a total drunk, he's also not particularly forthcoming with information," Mike commented.

"Details, please," I said.

"Every time we asked him about his wife and her alleged affair with Doug, he became hostile and then clammed up," Tommy said.

"Yeah," Mike added. "He started on this diatribe about how all that was in the past. She had left him for another man. She was gone and he didn't care—like that. Then nothing more. We could try to sweat him out, but this guy is such a drunk, I don't know whether he's even coherent enough for this crime—and he's not real bright either."

"Unfortunately, this crime didn't require a lot of brain cells," Tommy said, "so that in and of itself won't eliminate him from the suspect list." Tommy continued, "He's had a bunch of jobs in the last fourteen years since he moved to Manor from Viola. He's borderline in the job he has now, which he's only had for a month. He criticizes everybody and everything. He's basically not a very pleasant or happy fellow."

"His mother-in-law doesn't like him, that's for sure," Mike commented.

"That's not a reason to suspect a man," I said.

"We know that, Mom, but the guy is a lush, he's evasive and I get bad vibes from him."

"And everybody is on our list of suspects right now," Tommy added.

"Did he ever beat his wife?" I asked.

"We thought of that, Mom, and we asked around. The answer, even from his mother-in-law, was no."

"That's right. He was a real jerk to her, but no physical abuse."

"Sounds like you two have your work cut out for you," I said.

"Story of our lives," Tommy said, smiling.

"So, what's next, guys?"

"The standard stuff. I'd like to locate Doug Hughes, one way or the other," Tommy said. "Do a little more legwork on Dody Waldrep and Jimmy Hughes. Collect some more facts about the very unusual Lori Webster, and then see what shakes out of all that."

"Which reminds me, tell me about Lori Webster."

Gloria Hughes insisted that the rumors about Doug and Addie were just that. Yet the rumors persisted because of the attention Doug had paid to Addie and the fact he had been seen at the Waldrep home many times when Dody was not there. Vernon said that Doug had felt sorry for Addie because her husband was "a real heel." Still, it did seem odd that Doug would spend so much time maintaining a friendship with a married woman.

Mike and Tommy had followed up and gone to Georgetown, to talk with Lori. Lori had left town and moved about thirty miles away to Georgetown after Doug disappeared. In Mike and Tommy's book, Lori's move right after Doug's disappearance was unusual. That seemed to them like the actions of a guilty person. Mrs. Hughes told them that Lori had been "distraught" over Doug's disappearance and all the rumors about he and Addie, and that was why she left, but the boys didn't like it.

Lori had never married, and she had a job in a local department store in Georgetown, working as a customer service and credit clerk. Tommy and Mike had located her place of work in Georgetown from Gloria Hughes. Lori's family members still lived in Rock Hill and Viola, but had not seen Lori since she left sixteen years ago. She had not been back to visit any of them—another strange fact.

When they arrived at the store, Mike and Tommy had been shown back to the customer service office where Lori worked.

"They set us up in this little back room there," Tommy said, "and she came in and sat down with us."

"She was nervous and kneaded her hands and looked down at her feet a lot," Mike said.

"I broke the news to her, about finding Addie's remains in Austin. She was stunned, man, almost catatonic, never looked directly at either me or Mike."

"Yeah, then she burst into tears, which escalated into sobs. It was a strange reaction."

"When she collected herself a little, she says to me, 'Doug was found with her?'"

My eyes widened at Tommy, and he nodded his head.

"I know, I thought it was a strange way to word it, too. So I say, 'No, ma'am, we have not found Doug Hughes.'"

"Yeah, so she's sniffling and wiping her nose and her eyes, but she's focused on the wall to the right of her. Real weird."

Mike said that they proceeded to ask the woman all about her relationship with Doug. The rumors about he and Addie disturbed her, but she was sure that they were just rumors, and that his only interest in Addie was as a friend, just as his mother had said. Lori said when he disappeared, she was humiliated, hurt and unable to bear the gossip another moment, so she packed up and moved to Georgetown.

"That was the extent of what she told you?"

"Yeah," Tommy said. "And I know she's holding something back, because she doesn't look you in the eye when she talks, you know?"

"She's an odd one," Mike said. "She's off-kilter somehow—looking up at the wall when she talked, giving abbreviated answers to all of our questions, so that we had to pry every detail out of her."

"She has some really strange mannerisms," Tommy said. "Her eyes darted all over that wall, but she never looked at us. Other than her initial hysterical sobbing, her responses were all cool—disconnected. She had nervous movements, closed her eyes when she was talking to us..."

"Yeah, and the only other time she showed any emotion," Mike said, "was when she was talking about Addie. Then she became agitated and angry."

"She said Addie's name with jealousy attached to it," Tommy told me.

"A woman can shoot another woman in the head, dig a hole and bury her," Mike said.

"And a woman can dig up bones and rebury them," Tommy added.

"Do you think she could have killed them both?" I asked.

"Toni, I've seen everything in homicides, and I've seen women commit some pretty gruesome murders."

"Yeah, Mom, what about that wacko nurse who killed all those kids that time?"

"Okay. Point taken. If the woman is weird enough, anything is possible."

Then I told them both about the conversation I'd had with Leo about the crime. I told them everything she had told me.

"I even asked Leo if the killer could be a woman," I said.

"What'd she say?" Tommy asked.

"She said the killer could definitely be a woman, but that the stats say it's more likely to be a man."

"The things that Leo said could fit any of our suspects," Mike said.

"Yeah, I agree," Tommy said.

"The truth is here somewhere," I said.

After the graveside service in Viola, Mike and Tommy headed back to Austin. I stopped in at the local café for some lunch. Notice I said *the* local café, because one was all they had. Viola was so small, there wasn't even a Dairy Queen. The café was called the Main Street Café. Its proprietor was a sturdy-looking woman by the name of Doris. I knew her name was Doris because it was sewn onto the left breast pocket of the apron she wore.

I had seated myself at the counter and Doris approached me with a green plastic tumbler in one hand and a water pitcher in the other. Under the apron, Doris wore a cotton print dress. Her hair was bleached blond—probably to cover the gray—and teased up into the big-hair style. She had pudgy little hands and long fingernails polished expertly with red lacquer. Her lipstick matched her nail polish and, upon close inspection, I could see that Doris had run the lipstick just slightly outside of the natural edge of her lips. She couldn't have been more than five or six years older than me, but she seemed old enough to be my grandmother. In fact, she kind of reminded me of my grandmother.

"Hey there, hon. You're not from around here. Must be in town for Addie's funeral, right?"

"Well, yes," I said, just a little nonplussed. Then it occurred to me that this would be one of the few funerals they'd have in a town like this for a while, and as it involved murder and discovery of a missing woman sixteen years after her disappearance, this would be big doings indeed. Why else would an outsider stop in a small town like Viola, six miles off of the state highway, just to eat lunch?

"I don't recall ever seeing you before, hon. How did you know Addie?"

"Well, actually I never knew her in life. I'm the sculptor who reconstructed her face from her remains."

"Well, I say! You are, are you? Well, I say..."

She poured the water into the glass, shaking her head the whole time.

"Well, now, what can I get you for your lunch, hon?"

I gave Doris my order and she scratched it down on a little order pad she pulled out of her pocket, tore off the page and handed it through a small window behind the counter.

"There you go, Pop," she said to the man who was slaving over the stove.

Doris tended to several customers at the other end of the counter. Soon, two of them at the other end craned their necks around to look at me, and then whispered to Doris again. A few seconds later, Doris came back my way with the water pitcher. She was smiling and popping chewing gum between her teeth.

"You know, hon, I saw that sculpture you did on the news the other night. I knew as soon as I seen it that it was her. You just did a wonderful job—a wonderful job. How'd you do such a great job of making that look like little Addie?"

I explained to her about the anthropological charts and about what I do to try to make the reconstruction as personal and human as I can. She listened intently, nodding the whole time and alternately smacking and then popping her gum.

"Well," she said when I was done with my explanation, "you just did a wonderful job." Then she sighed appreciatively.

I thanked her and she turned around to get my sandwich out of the pass-through window where Pop had put it. She laid it on the counter in front of me and winked as she walked away.

The sandwich was delicious. It consisted of cheese, tomatoes, lettuce, onions and Doris's special dressing on whole wheat bread. On the menu it came with ham, but as I'm a vegetarian, I had asked Doris to omit that. As I licked my lips over the last couple of bites, Doris revisited my section of the counter.

"How was it, hon?"

"Mmm, fantastic," I said while still chewing the last bite.

"How about some of my homemade pie?"

"Oh, I don't know..."

"Oh, hon, you have to have some of my home-made pie. We have chocolate cream today and apple. Everyone just raves about them both, but my favorite is the apple."

"Well, okay, I'll have the apple."

"You want ice cream on it, hon?"

"No, thank you."

When Doris cut you a piece of pie, Doris cut you a slab of pie. I have lived in Texas my whole life and I don't recall ever seeing a piece of pie that large, not even at my grandma's house.

Doris hung over the edge of the counter waiting for me to take the first bite. That pie was heaven in a crust.

"Oh my!" I exclaimed.

Of course, Doris was delighted at my reaction.

"Well, I'm sure glad you like it all that well. That just makes me feel so good." She bumped the heel of her hand on the edge of the counter for punctuation.

As was typical in a small town in Texas, the owner of the local café knew just about everybody and everything going on in town and the surrounding area. I decided to find out just how much information I could get from Doris.

"So, Doris, how well did you know Addie?"

"Oh, hon, I knew her and Dody their whole lives. Why, Dody's about eight years younger than me and I can remember when he was born. My little brother used to play with him."

"I see."

"Addie was a lot younger. Her birthday was just a week before mine. I always remembered that because she was born right before my sweet-sixteen party." Doris beamed at the memory.

"Well, how about that?" I said.

"Yes. Mama and Daddy had a party out at the house and Daddy churned homemade ice cream and Mama made pie—that very recipe that I used to make the pie you're eating right now!"

"Oh, well, what a treat."

"Yes, it was. Mama and Daddy invited everyone in town to my party—everyone! It was wonderful. Pop was there, too." She pointed back at Pop in the kitchen.

"Oh, really?"

"Why, yes. Pop was my sweetheart from high school."

Then she began to tell me how Addie and Dody had begun dating when Addie was sixteen. Dody was already twenty-four by then and some people in the town were wondering if he would ever settle down. They thought Addie was too young for him, or at least too young to know what she was doing. He and Addie did marry, though, and had two children, Melissa and Emma.

"They sound like such a happy family," I remarked. "I wouldn't have thought that Addie would run off with someone, the way you describe her."

"Well, she and Dody only got along because Addie wouldn't talk back to him. I think that's one reason why Dody wanted to marry someone so young—so he wouldn't be challenged. I tell you, I'd have never put up with his nonsense."

"What do you mean?"

"He was unreasonable as he could be. Grumpy, just grumpy. Didn't like anything anybody did or the way they did it. I think Addie met Doug and just saw her savior."

"A way to get out of the relationship with Dody."

"Right. And you know, Addie and Doug could never have had a relationship and stayed here."

"So, she left her kids and everything?"

"Well, that kind of surprised me, but I reckon if she'd taken them with her and all, there would have been big problems. Living through a divorce like that in a small town like this..." Doris shuddered.

"Why are you so sure that they were actually having an affair? I mean, did people actually see them together?"

"I didn't, but I heard that other people saw them talking and looking very secretive in their talk. Also, Doug came by the house when Dody wasn't there. In fact, he never did come by at all if Dody was home."

"Couldn't just have been because Dody was so unpleasant?"

She turned up one corner of her mouth. "Well...I guess it could, but why would he be dropping by the house of a married woman like that? I don't know...I suppose it could be like you say, but that just doesn't make sense to me."

"Yeah, I see what you mean. So, tell me more about Doug—what kind of guy was he?"

"He was a nice fella. I know his mama. You know Rock Hill is only about ten miles from here and it's smaller than Viola. They don't have no café over there."

I nodded.

"Doug's mother has always sworn that her son wouldn't have had an affair with Addie. She always said that they were friends and she knew he wouldn't do that, but you know, she's his mother, so what would you think she'd say?"

"She would know him real well."

"Well, I know, hon, but still she wouldn't be wanting to think her boy would do something like that even if he was guilty of it, now, would she?"

"Did she have anything to back up what she said?"

"She claimed that Doug was just being friendly to Addie and all because he felt sorry for her—on account of Dody being so hard to live with. She said that Doug was sweet on some girl in Rock Hill—I forget her name now—but, anyway, none of us ever saw him with anybody, so I always just dismissed that as his mama's wishful thinkin'."

"Think he could have killed Addie?"

"Doug? Oh, my! I just don't see that. I mean, I think Doug would have run off with her, but I just can't imagine that he killed her."

"So, what do you think happened?"

"Well, hon, I think maybe they broke up after they left here, and she just fell into the hands of the wrong person."

"You don't think Dody could have done it?"

"Well, I don't know. If he did, he'd have had to kill both of them. I just can't imagine Dody being a killer. He's contrary and he's kind of an oddball sometimes, but I think he's basically harmless. I mean, he was always hard on Addie, but he never did lay hands on her—you know, hit her or anything. If he had, the whole town would have known about that. I mean, you can't get a hangnail 'round here without everybody knowing."

"I've heard that Doug's mother hasn't heard from him since the time he disappeared with Addie. Is that true?"

"Oh yes, that is true. I've often wondered about that myself. Perhaps he and Addie were both killed out on the road somewhere and we just haven't found his bones yet."

"Hmm. Perhaps." We both paused for a few seconds. "So, what happened with Dody and the girls after she left?" I took another huge bite of pie.

"Oh well, he was never the same person again. That's another reason I don't think he could have killed them. When she ran off, he just kind of came apart. I mean, he was still negative and all, but he hardly ever talked to folks. He withdrew, kind of. Had a lot of stomach problems—ulcers, you know." She looked at me knowingly and nodded.

"I see."

"Yes," she continued. "Ulcers and then with all his drinkin'—he started that after she run off—with all his drinkin' on top of those ulcers..." She made a soft clicking noise with her tongue behind her teeth.

"Then he left about fourteen years ago?"

"Yes, to move to Manor, but those little girls spent most of their time with their grandmother anyway—Addie's mama—Dody's mama passed away some years ago."

"Well, it just all seems so sad."

"Yes, it does," Doris sighed.

I paid her for the lunch and that awesome pie and headed back to Austin. On the way, I pondered everything I had seen and everything Doris had told me, and I wondered what had befallen Addie and Doug after they had left Viola, or if they had ever left Viola. I wanted to know if she had really been involved with Doug. I wanted to know what had really happened.

I was packing my clothes for the trip to Hawaii. All of my sculpture supplies were already packed in a case that I would carry with me on the trip. I was standing in the doorway to my closet trying to decide what final pieces of my wardrobe I would take with me, when I heard the front door open.

"Mom?"

"I'm back here—in my closet."

I heard Mike's heavy footsteps coming across the living room floor and then down the hallway. I looked up to see my son standing in the door to my room. He was wearing jeans and a golf shirt with the tail out.

"What are you doing here, son?"

"I came over to take you to the airport. You're not through packing yet?"

"You don't have to take me to the airport."

"Of course I don't, but that's beside the point. I am taking you to the airport. Mom, your flight leaves in three hours. I thought you'd be done packing."

"Thought wrong, but I am almost done. I just need to make a decision on one more thing..."

He sighed. It was one of those deep, male, "I totally don't get this" kind of sighs. I finally selected one of my favorite sundresses. I removed it from the hanger, folded it neatly and placed it in my bag. Then I closed the top and zipped the bag up. I was done.

"There."

"You're done?"

"Yes. I told you I only needed one more thing."

"So, your supplies are already packed? Please tell me that your supplies are already packed."

"Yes, Michael. I packed those four days ago."

"Good."

"So, why did you decide you needed to take me to the airport?"

"For one thing, you don't need to be leaving one of the cars out there for several days. Grandpa doesn't need to be driving you out there either—the traffic is awful, and he gets hacked off with the way people drive. I'm off today, and what kind of a son would I be if I didn't take my mom to the airport?"

I gave him one of my looks and raised my left eyebrow.

"You're a lousy storyteller, Michael Sullivan."

He looked down at his feet.

"I didn't want to send you off to do something like this without moral support. I don't want you coming back from this trip and having to drive yourself home alone either."

I nodded.

"You're a pretty decent son, Michael Sullivan." I smiled and then patted him on the arm.

"Don't go gettin' mushy on me or anything, Mom."

"Oh no, I wouldn't dream of that."

We both grinned at each other. I looked up at my only child and marveled. He was six feet one inch tall, and with his strawberry-blond hair and blue eyes he was the spitting image of my husband. Now he was in the same line of work as Jack, too. Now my little boy was a big man who carried a badge and a gun. Then I couldn't help myself, and I reached up and put my arms around the neck of my "little" boy. My son whom I used to hold in my arms when he cried. My son whose boo-boos I used to kiss and assure him everything was okay. Then something incredible happened.

"It's all going to be okay, Mom." He squeezed me tight. "I'm here for you, and we'll get through this thing with Uncle Teddy together."

Tears were streaming down my face. I had not intended to lean on my son for support through this, but without my asking or saying so much as a single word, here he was. I wept because it was the first time my small boy had changed roles and become the man to buck up his ol' ma.

He pulled away from me and pulled his hankie out of his pocket. "No more of that cryin' now. Wipe your face, and let's get your stuff loaded in the car and get on the road. You're the best in your field, and you've faced worse things in life than this. You can do this. Let's get going."

Chapter Nine

The flight from Austin had been uneventful. The plane landed on the tarmac in Honolulu and I looked out the window to see Hawaii. I hadn't been here in a couple of years, since the last reconstruct I did for CILHI. Every time I came here it reminded me of Vietnam—not because of CILHI, but because I had stopped here on my way home from Vietnam. Jack and I had pulled one of our R&Rs here, too. Hawaii would be forever associated with Vietnam in my mind, but no post-Vietnam visit here had resurrected feelings and memories associated with 'Nam like this visit had.

I had taken a hotel on the beach at Waikiki. I thought, Why not? I have to go to Hawaii for unpleasant business, I can stay in a nice hotel. I hadn't been on a trip anywhere for pleasure since before Jack died, and this trip definitely didn't count toward that deficiency, but at least the view was extraordinary and the weather was amazing.

I had checked in to the hotel and was in my room unpacking some things and looking out the sliding glass door that led out onto the lanai. The beauty of the place was in such incredible contrast to what I was there to do. I didn't have to report to CILHI until the next day, so I had the rest of the afternoon and evening to get settled in and to collect myself.

I had noticed that there was a luau planned downstairs that night and I decided that I would go. As a vegetarian, I didn't relish the idea of watching people eat a roasted animal, but I could steer myself toward the vegetables and just sit outdoors in the pleasant evening air and eat. In any event, it beat sitting alone in the room eating room-service food.

After I unpacked some of my things, I took a hot shower and refreshed myself. I got my makeup on just right, and fluffed my short hair up with the help of a blow-dryer and a little styling gel. I pulled out a brightly colored tropical-print sundress that I brought over for just something like this. Once I had the dress on and my hair just so, I slid my feet into some nice little dress sandals I had brought with me, and headed downstairs for a dinner to take my mind off of everything except paradise.

* * *

The luau food had been good, but I sat as far away from the hapless pig as possible. A very nice couple from Saint Louis sat next to me and we had a great conversation, which diverted my attention from the duties of the next morning.

That morning couldn't have been a more beautiful morning—a morning in paradise. I decided to wear my dark green slacks and a light green raw-silk shirt with my dress sandals from the night before. I needed to be comfortable and wear something in which I could do my work, but I also wanted to make a good impression on the military personnel and the scientists with whom I would be spending my time that day.

I was dressed and ready to go by 8:00 a.m. It was a thirty-minute cab ride from the hotel to Hickham Air Force Base, the home of CILHI. I rode with the windows down, relishing the tropical breeze along the way. One of the benefits of having short hair is that it's virtually impossible to really mess it up. I definitely had hair suitable for windows-down or top-down, depending on the vehicle.

We got through the gate at the base and arrived at the steps of the CILHI labs, where I paid the cabbie and sent him on his way.

Once inside the front doors, I checked in and waited for Sergeant Major Tomlinson. In a couple of minutes the sergeant major appeared from around a corner and walked down the hall toward me. If there was even a slight wrinkle in his uniform I couldn't see it. His uniform always astounded me.

His hair was cut so short that it was hard to tell if it was sandy-colored blond or brown. One thing was certain, however; his eyes were deep blue, with a twinkle in them that belied his military bearing.

We shook hands, I picked up my case and we proceeded down the hall to one of the work areas. Once there, I greeted anthropologists whom I had met before and was introduced to several new ones.

I put my case on an empty table they had set aside for me. One of the new anthropologists to whom I was introduced was Dr. Sean Carroway, who would be working with me on "Ted's case." The sergeant major excused himself saying that he would return when I was ready to leave later that day.

Dr. Carroway was an interesting guy. He wore a nice pair of trousers and a plaid shirt under a white lab coat, but when I looked down at his feet, I noticed he was wearing hiking boots. He was about five foot eight with a slight frame. I imagined he was about thirty-five years old. He had a shock of wavy, ash-blond hair and dark brown eyes. When he smiled, his eyes crinkled at the corners and his left eyebrow would lift slightly. He was a serious scientist, but I imagined there was a bit of a mischievous streak in him. He had a deep, resonant voice that had a soothing, almost mesmerizing quality to it. That was a good thing, since I was sure I was going to be appreciative of anything soothing in a few moments.

Dr. Carroway and I chatted for a while, becoming familiar with each other. We discussed our education and experience, and he asked me about the two other cases I had worked on at CILHI, which predated his tenure there.

When we had finished the preliminaries, Carroway retrieved the box containing the remains in question. He laid the box on the table in front of us and lifted the lid. I held my breath. I remembered when Jack had died how I had dreaded that first moment when I saw his body after death. These were just fragments of bones, but I dreaded seeing them nonetheless. I felt my stomach tighten slightly. As the lid slipped away from the top of the box, I looked down.

Inside was the skull that had been put back together and numerous pieces of bones, none of which were larger than two inches in length. Most were about half an inch to an inch long. There were only about twenty pieces in the entire box. The skull had a piece missing out of the back and part of the lower jaw was gone, but I could still do the facial reconstruction with what was there. Overall, it was as bad as I had feared. If these were indeed the remains of my friend...well, I already began to feel sick that there should be no more left of Ted Nikolaides than this. I hadn't been able to eat breakfast that morning and I was glad; otherwise, I think I would have thrown up.

I exhaled, gutted up and lifted the skull out of the box. When my fingers actually touched the bone, I shivered inside. It was all I could do to maintain my control.

Dr. Carroway spoke. "Dr. Sullivan, I understand you knew the man to whom we suspect these remains belong. Is that true?"

"Yes. He was a pilot in Da Nang when I was a nurse there. My late husband and I knew him."

I set the skull down on the table. I was glad to take my hands off of it for a moment.

"So, is there anything else you need me to get for you?" Dr. Carroway asked.

"No. I brought all my supplies."

"What is the first step? Do you mind if I stay and observe?"

I was relieved he wanted to stay and observe. As strange as it may sound, I didn't want to be alone in the room with those remains.

"I don't mind at all if you stay. In answer to your question, the first step is to prepare the material that I'll use for the mold. It's kind of like what the dentist does when making an impression of your teeth."

I opened the case I had brought with me. Inside was the form into which I would place the plastic material for the mold. I had designed it myself for use in my work. A machinist friend of mine had fashioned it from my design using lightweight aluminum. I was a good welder, but I didn't have the skills for heli-arc welding, and that's what it took to weld aluminum.

The form looked like a head and shoulders, but it opened in half and the inside was hollow. The hollow area inside the form was larger than a human head would be. The plastic molding material would be placed in this hollow and the skull would then be pressed into the front half of the material, and the back half of the form would be closed over the back of the skull. I would leave it there long enough for the plastic material to firm up and harden.

The skull could then be lifted out of the material and I would have a mold into which I could pour plaster, so that I would have a cast of the skull onto which I could add clay "flesh." I explained all of the process to Dr. Carroway as I began to prepare the mold for the skull.

"So, how do you know how the nose looks?" he asked.

"The human face has amazing proportions," I explained. "The length of the nose is proportionate to the length of the eyes. The length of the eyes can be calculated by the size of the orbits—" the sockets in the bone where the eyes are located. "You use the orbits to calculate where the ligaments for the eyelids go and to determine the size and shape of the eyes."

"Yes, of course," he said. "So, once you have that done, it gives you an idea of the nose length?"

"Yes, and the nose bone shows the height of the nose and the shape of its ridge. If any of the cartilage is left there, it just makes it that much easier. Also, the inner edge of the iris in the eye gives me the width of the nose at the nostrils, and the exterior edge of the iris in the eye shows the ends of the mouth. The brow ridge in the bone defines the eyebrows over the eyes."

"It all fits together proportionately."

"Yes."

"It's science."

"Yes, and it's the hand of the Creator—an intelligent design."

"Well, I'm a man of science myself."

"I'm a woman of science. I believe that science is a tool the Creator gives us to better understand His creation. I see no conflict between the two."

"That's an interesting perspective. You said the design was intelligent. Why couldn't it be chance—the laws of nature."

"When Frank Lloyd Wright designed a magnificent building or home where the design itself evoked an emotional response in those who viewed it, and where all of the angles and proportions seemed to fit together, melding art and function in an amazing way, people oohed and aahed and said, 'Wow, what an amazing design. What genius!' Do you doubt for a moment that the house or building was designed in an intelligent way, and that the design itself reflects that fact?"

"No," he said tentatively.

"Yet these designs pale in comparison to the designs in nature, and in particular to the design of the human body, and we want to deny the genius there? We want to deny the intelligence behind the design?"

"You make an interesting point, Dr. Sullivan."

"I think the design not only bears absolute testimony to the intelligence and the supreme genius of the Designer, I think that there is a real correlation, or harmony, between our ability to design and create, and the fact that He who created us also designs and creates. This is all the internal part of the image of Himself in us."

"Wow. I like that very much—what you're saying about the harmony of creative talents between us and the Creator. So, you're saying that He has this ability, and in a lesser sense He gave us the same ability."

"Yes—within our human limitations."

"Then you re-create that image in your work, Dr. Sullivan." He smiled broadly now.

"No, Dr. Carroway, I only restore an idea of the physical part of that image. The most essential part of the image in us can only be re-created by the Master Himself."

"Requires a higher power, then, eh?"

"Requires a sacred touch," I said.

Dr. Carroway nodded his head.

"I like that. I'll have to think about it more when you're gone."

"Good."

"But I may have lots more questions for you later," he said, winking.

I winked back, and said, "Bring them on and I'll do my best to give you proper answers."

While we waited for the material to firm up around the skull, Dr. Carroway offered to show me the personal effects they had found with or near the remains.

He retrieved another box and opened the lid. Inside was part of a dog-tag chain with no dog tags, an American quarter, a button off of a flight suit and part of the pilot's helmet. None of it was absolutely personal to Teddy. I picked up the button, turned it over in the palm of my hand and wondered. I put the button back into the box and picked up the piece of dog-tag chain.

All I could think of was what had probably happened to all the things that weren't found with the remains. Of course, the flight suit and all the fabrics he was wearing would have burned, or deteriorated and biodegraded. Villagers carried off parts of the plane, jewelry and American dog tags. Wild animals would have carried off other things, and that's what

I just couldn't think about now. I wanted to sit down and cry, but that wasn't exactly a professional response. The segment of dog-tag chain slipped through my fingers back into the box.

When I looked up at Dr. Carroway again, he had a sympathetic expression on his face. My expression must have been more transparent than I thought.

I looked back down at the box of personal effects and said, "Well, none of it is absolutely identifiable as something that would have belonged to Niko-laides."

"No," he said softly.

If the situation continued that way, I knew that I would not be able to retain my composure, so I changed the subject—rapidly.

"Well, let's check the mold and see how we're doing."

I walked back to the table where the form lay, and I put my finger in the bottom of it to check the consistency of the plastic material. It wasn't ready yet.

"Not quite yet," I said, praying he wouldn't want to discuss anything relating to Ted personally.

"So, Dr. Sullivan, tell me how you got into this line of work. I know you were an artist, but how and why did you come to this work after being a nurse in the war?"

I could have hugged him.

"When I came home from 'Nam, the last thing I wanted to do was nursing. Other nurses felt differently and continued, but I couldn't. So, I went back to school and got my art degrees. Art was my true love, so that part of it was a natural choice."

"After getting out of nursing, why did you choose to go into something…well, that takes you into dealing with death again."

"Good question. What I saw in 'Nam was a lot of horror, but it was bloody horror, and it was human suffering. Forensic art and sculpture isn't bloody and the suffering is already past, at least for the departed. I don't take care of the families or friends of the victims, so it's totally different to me."

Suddenly, I could hear Reverend Iordani's words to me replaying in my head, and it hit me hard. I must have looked as if I was drifting off, because Dr. Carroway interrupted my thoughts again.

"So, you said your husband was a police officer. I'm assuming that's what led you into this."

"Yes, it is. Jack used to discuss his tough cases with me, and I had a knack for helping him solve them—an artist's eye for details, I guess. Anyway, we were exposed to this new science of forensic reconstructive art, and I decided I wanted to learn it. I spent some time with two really terrific forensic reconstructive artists, and then began to do some work on my own. My artistic credentials and my husband's connections allowed me access to the right people to teach me the skills."

"Now you're one of the best in the country."

"Well, I don't know about that..."

"No, Dr. Sullivan, you are regarded as one of the very best in the country. I checked."

I felt myself blushing. I looked down at my feet, cleared my throat and said, "Well, I work hard and enjoy what I do."

The material in the form was firmed up, so I cut the form open and gently lifted the skull out of the impression. It was a good impression. It would now harden fully and I could transport it back to Austin where the remainder of the work could take place.

"Wow, that's really interesting," Dr. Carroway remarked, looking at the fresh mold.

"Yes, the mold looks good."

"Have you ever had one turn out bad?"

I laughed. "Oh yeah. That's when you ditch it and start all over."

We both smiled.

I packed up all my supplies, and Dr. Carroway called the sergeant major, who escorted me out of the building to my waiting cab. On my way back to the hotel, the memories of 'Nam began to flood in.

The first horror that revisited my mind was the smell. You never forget the smell and it's something you really can't describe. It's sour and stale—a decayed smell. It was the smell that came with blood, burn wounds, infections and death. It'll wrench your gut up into your throat. As if the smell wasn't bad enough, the images that come along with it finish you off and you're retching and in the dry heaves in no time flat. I already felt sick after my morning at the CILHI labs. The remembrance of that smell was compounding my queasiness. The remembrance of it was so real, it was as if it was there in the cab with me.

The dentists had the worst duty. The mortuary was nearby and a lot of the dead were burn victims—napalm and air crashes on the landing strip. They had to be identified by dental records. Those poor dentists would throw up three or four times just doing the ID on one body. I don't know how any of them ever ate anything while they were in 'Nam.

None of that was even the worst part of the war. I was a nurse in the air force. The army nurses in the MASH units and evac hospitals—those women must have lost their minds or nearly so. They saw everything that came off the battlefield. The worst wounded usually never made it my way because they were never in good enough shape for plane flight. In fact, they usually died before they made it to our hospital.

I was in charge of triaging the injured for plane transport to another hospital, Hawaii or maybe even back home. The ones who were really bad couldn't go on a plane, although that didn't keep some doctors from trying to get them on one. There was no way to pressurize a plane for ground-level pressure.

The best that could be achieved was pressure equal to three thousand or four thousand feet. You need more oxygen than that for certain wounds, especially burns and eye wounds. Oxygen tanks were not something we had in abundance, so there was triage. I would do an evaluation of their condition for plane flight. The ones who didn't qualify had to go back to a hospital nearby to improve their condition, or just to die and return home in a box.

The bad news is that I saw a lot of horrible stuff. The good news is that I never had a patient more than twenty-four hours. It was an assessment assembly line and I was charged with making some difficult decisions in short order.

I met Jack there in Vietnam. He was an MP who did duty on the perimeter at the base where I was stationed in Da Nang. He used to play cards and hang out with that flyboy named Teddy Nikolaides. Teddy, Jack and I became a tight trio. We'd sit around and talk about home and dreams—and Teddy's wife and kids.

Jack and I saw a lot of our buddies go into battle or fly off the airstrip and never return, but no loss hit us as hard as the loss of Ted Nikolaides. I don't think either one of us ever really got our head around that one.

Ted had almost made it out of that horrible place—almost. I wondered now if he had finally made it out. Were the fragments I had seen and the skull I had touched really all that was left of Ted? Had he finally made it home to American soil?

Back at the hotel I secured the case with the skull mold in it and took a long hot shower. I put on fresh clothes—blue-jean shorts, a white cotton tank top and sandals. I was going to do what I had done each of the two previous times I had been to Hawaii since the Vietnam War. I was taking a trip to the Hawaii National Cemetery of the Pacific—to the Punchbowl.

The Punchbowl is the bowl-shaped remains of a volcanic crater just north of downtown Honolulu. In Hawaiian, the name for this place means "Hill of Sacrifice." There are over thirty-three-thousand veterans buried in the floor of the crater. A memorial at the head of the cemetery consists of ten Courts of the Missing—marble courts containing the names of the MIAs from World War II, the Korean War and Vietnam—more than twenty-eight-thousand of them in all. In one of those Courts of the Missing, engraved on a marble wall, was the name of Theodore P. Nikolaides.

I would leave Hawaii for Austin the next morning, but first I would make my traditional trip to the Punchbowl, the Hill of Sacrifice, to find my friend's name in the Courts of the Missing, and I would pay my respects.

✄ *Chapter Ten* ✄

Heavily jet-lagged and back in my house less than two hours, I received a call from Chris. There were more bones. This time not far from the edge of the running trail and the bridge that crosses Waller Creek. I taped my eyelids open, put on some jeans and boots and threw on an old, khaki-colored Keep Austin Weird T-shirt and bolted out the door.

It hadn't been started in four days, but the 'Stang fired up like the little land rocket it was. As I roared down the road, I wondered what in blazes was going on. Could this victim be Doug Hughes?

I called my son on the cell phone. He was at the scene and he and Tommy were working this case as if it was related to the Red Bud case, until they could prove otherwise. He said the bones were in a jumble as with the Red Bud case, and it looked like a fresh grave.

It was 7:00 a.m. and traffic was already getting heavy, but I put the pedal down as I pulled up onto IH-35. As I wove in and out of traffic, speeding up, gearing down and shifting lanes, a motorcycle cop pulled alongside me. I just knew he was going to pull me over, but he motioned for me to follow him. That son of mine, always thinking. I smiled to myself as the officer turned on his lights and sirens and the traffic parted before us like the Red Sea before Moses.

We flew down the highway to the Cesar Chavez off-ramp. The officer's Harley maneuvered easily through traffic as we continued our wild ride across downtown Austin, finally turning in at the parking area next to the old power plant on the riverbank. I thanked the officer for his escort and he smiled and waved as he pulled away.

Waller Creek fed into Town Lake here, and the running trails that banked the river crossed the creek via a wooden pedestrian bridge. I made my way down the trail to the grim group that had gathered near that bridge. As I walked up, I smiled at my son.

"That escort your idea?"

He chuckled and nodded. "I thought you might appreciate that. Besides, Mario, I know you and I didn't want my mother getting pulled over for speeding or running down pedestrians with that hot rod you drive."

"You are a good son." I winked and patted him on the back.

I walked up to Chris Nakis, who stood in her usual dapper attire and lab coat, looking more serious than ever.

"What's the word here?" I asked.

"Bad." She shook her head. "Real scary bad. Two sets of bones in as many weeks." She looked up at me, and our eyes met.

"I called Leo," I told her. "It's her day off, but I told her I wanted her down here. I want her to see this. I'll bet this is Doug Hughes."

"Who?"

"Lover of the first victim. They disappeared at the same time sixteen years ago. It just makes sense it would be him."

"Hmm. That's interesting."

"What do you know so far?"

"Not much, just that the bones are old and the grave is fresh. The guys are digging carefully so as not to disturb any evidence."

"It's too much of a coincidence not to be related to the other case."

"Yes, I agree."

While Mike and Tommy questioned the woman who had found the "body," Chris and I stood and watched as one of the forensic anthropologists worked on unearthing a bone.

"So, I heard you made a quick trip to Hawaii," Chris said.

"How'd you know about that?"

"Mike told me."

"Then he told you why I made the trip?"

"Yes. So, how did it go?"

"I made the mold I needed."

Chris cleared her throat. "The skull was in good shape then?"

"Well, it was in five or six pieces, but one of the CILHI anthropologists had put it back together so I could work with it."

"And the rest of the remains?"

"Not much to it. Less than twenty pieces of bone, one to two inches long."

Chris looked down at her feet.

I continued. "The only DNA that's usable is mitochondrial. None of Ted's maternal family is alive or locatable now. The only thing the DNA was good for was matching all the pieces together. So, when I'm done, if the image is Ted's, they'll know all the remains belong to him."

Chris nodded. "Well, you know if you need me for anything... I'm not sure what I could do, but if you need me..."

"Thanks."

Leo's Jeep screeched to a stop in the parking lot

at the top of the bank. She bailed out and came jogging down the trail toward our position. When she got to the site, Chris filled her in on the details as she knew them.

Leo approached the site carefully to get a closer look. As she squatted next to one of the forensic anthropologists, he lifted an arm bone out of the dirt. He carefully bagged it and handed it to a forensic tech who was logging everything and laying all the separate bags into a black body bag. Leo stood up, stepped back and took in a wider view of the site. She looked out over the water with her hands on her hips. I saw the familiar trance come over her face. She stood that way for a minute or so and then shook her head as if she was shaking something off. She stepped over to where Chris and I were standing. Tommy and Mike joined us.

"What?" I asked.

"Nothing more than what I told you the other day," Leo said. "Remember what I told you?"

"Yes," I said. "But I was hoping you'd have more to add this time."

"No more to add. It still feels the same, except for one thing."

"So, elaborate."

"I said before I thought the killer wanted to get rid of the victim without being responsible for getting rid of her. There's something different here."

"Why does someone do this?" Chris asked.

"You mean, the reburial action?" Leo asked.

"Exactly."

Leo shook her head. "I don't know for sure, but I feel a real purpose in this one. He wanted this one found. So, the burning question now is—why? Why did this one need to be found?"

"What makes you so sure this one *was* supposed to be found?" Tommy asked.

Leo turned and spread her hands out over the scene. "Look at it. The body is next to the running trail. It's on high ground, there's no coverage from brush or trees—there's not a snowball's chance in August this body was going to wash down into the creek or the river. People jog by here all the time— it was only a matter of time before the dirt shifted enough to reveal bone. The only thing more obvious would be leaving it on the trail, but then the coons or other animals might carry parts off."

"Okay, okay," Tommy said. "I see all that, but maybe he thought he buried the bones deep enough, or maybe he just wasn't thinking clearly."

"No," Leo said. "Look at the scene, Tommy. This is out in the wide open, next to the trail, on this little ridge above the creek. There's no way you hide a body here. The other one was buried on Red Bud Isle in a heavily wooded area, on the opposite side from where people crossing the bridge would see it, and in the path of the waters coming out of the floodgates. He was thinking—boy, was he thinking...but what, why? Why did he hide the first one and bury this one in plain sight?"

Leo and I were both hooked on this case. The finding of more bones that morning left us with more unanswered questions than before. After we left the scene at Waller Creek, Leo wanted to go to Red Bud Isle and actually walk the scene there. I agreed. She followed me in her Jeep and we parked in a small gravel-covered parking area just off the road. As we got out of our vehicles we heard a soft splashing sound. I looked, and rowing downriver on the other side of the isle was a canoeist with a long gray ponytail. Leo caught it, too. I shuddered and looked at her.

"Interesting."

"Could he be visiting the burial site."

"Could be, or he could just be rowing on the river like he said he does."

"This is a ways upriver from the rental place."

"True. But this is also where everybody else rows when they rent those canoes."

"I don't like it."

"I didn't say I did either, just saying it's possible that it's nothing."

We walked through the thick foliage on the isle down to the edge that faced the Tom Miller Dam. There was another small islet off to the right, but straight in front of us was the silent wall of the dam.

The day was overcast, but there was no rain, and it was cool and still. There were few birds out, and it seemed unusually quiet in that spot. The crime scene tape had been removed, but the area from which the bones had been recovered was barren—devoid of vegetation—the red-clay surface bearing the scars of Addie Waldrep's second grave. A blue heron, startled by our arrival, departed from a log floating near the other small islet, and flew gracefully past the end of Red Bud Isle as he ascended along the face of the limestone cliffs.

Leo stopped near the water's edge and looked down at the naked grave site. Then she looked up and around at that end of the isle. She turned and looked back in the direction from which we had come. She stood thinking for a moment and then turned and faced the mighty dam, and with her hands on her hips she stood like that for several minutes. I said nothing.

Finally she spoke. "This wasn't the reason the killer went back."

"What do you mean?"

"This victim—she wasn't the reason he went back. He went back to where they were buried because of the one we found today. That was his purpose—whatever it was, that was his purpose."

"What makes you say that?"

"Because there was purpose in it. This one I think he took and reburied just because he was there. He went there for the victim we found this morning, but for some reason he just decided to take her, too, and be rid of her. He just couldn't bring himself to dump her."

"So, he buried her here and thought she'd wash away."

Leo nodded. "Look at this place. The edge of it is soaked in water right now."

Leo was wearing jeans and a lightweight sweat-shirt, and sturdy hiking boots. The water lapped up against the edge of her right foot. The area where Addie had been buried was damp.

"The water has been up over this spot already," Leo said. "They must have had more than one gate open last night."

I nodded.

"How would the killer know to come exactly to this place?"

We both looked at each other. We stood in silence for a moment.

"So, what do you think the purpose was in ex-posing the victim we found this morning?"

"Don't know, but it's too obvious. That had to be his main purpose. When we find out who that vic-tim is, we may be able to figure all this out. But this...I believe this was secondary."

The water lapped up around Leo's feet.

Leo broke the silence first. "So what's up with your Vietnam case?"

I sighed and ran my hand through my hair.

"Tommy told me you went to Hawaii to start the work on the restoration of the MIA."

"That's right," I said. "I'm still pretty jet-lagged, too."

"So, how did it all go?"

"It was difficult. I handled the skull of someone I might have known over thirty years ago. I've never done a reconstruct on someone I knew, and I wouldn't do one under any other circumstance. I've thought a lot about Ted lately, his last days, and about Jack."

"I know you miss Jack. He was a cool guy."

"Yeah, he was. Sometimes it's hard for me to even realize that he's not here anymore. If I think about it too much—remember him *too* well—it overwhelms me."

"I understand that totally. It isn't romantic for me, like it is for you, but I feel that same kind of awful reality when I think too much about Bobby."

It was the first time since Bobby Driskill's death I had heard Leo mention her brother by his name.

"When Bobby was alive, everything was different. In a way it was easier for me because he took care of everything, and I could just be the little sister. Pete tries, but he's so laid-back, so different from Bobby— and that's not a bad thing. Pete has to be Pete. I love him just like he is. It's just that I have to be a grown-up now." She smiled. "Pete barely qualifies as one."

"Tommy is strong, though."

"Tommy and I are still trying to rebuild what we had, and then move on from there. Trying to repair ourselves—individually and together. He just blamed himself so much when Bobby got shot. He still struggles with it. I can tell him it's okay—and it is, as far as I'm concerned—but I can't really help him because I still have my own grief. I think he misunderstands that sometimes. It has nothing to do with him, but I think he feels like it does."

I nodded. This is why she doesn't sleep, I thought.

"How often do you talk openly with him about it?" I asked.

"I guess not very often. We both work a lot. Our cases take so much of our time and energy. When I work with him on a case—like the warehouse fire— it's difficult to do my job the way I know I need to and tend to his needs at the same time."

"All the more reason to set aside time to be up front with him, Leo."

"I know, Toni, but it's easier for you than it is for me. That kind of directness is just part of your nature. I have to really work at it."

I smiled and put my hand on her shoulder. "If there's anything I can do to help..."

"Just talking to you helps."

"Good," I said. "That's what friends are for. Now, what's the latest on your warehouse fire?"

She smiled. "I brought that big fat liar in for questioning and spent hours just grilling him. The forensic shrink gave me some good tips on how to handle him. I Mirandized him first, he declined counsel, and another investigator and I went after him. We videotaped the whole thing from start to finish so nobody could say we didn't do it right. Finally, the squatty-bodied little runt caved. He admitted the whole thing. He knew the type of accelerant used and everything."

"Excellent!"

"Yeah." She grinned, then her grin began to fade a bit. "Tommy was furious, though. He and Mike were sure the other guy was the one. I knew that my suspect was trying to make him look guilty. Anyway, I didn't do it to make Tommy look bad. I discussed it with both of them before I went forward. I offered to let them participate, but they blew me off."

"Well, then, let the chips fall where they may, Leo. My son and his partner are big boys. They made that decision and it turned out not to be a very good one. That's not your fault. Nice work on your part. You stopped a pyromaniac and killer, and kept an innocent man from being falsely accused."

"Yeah." She grinned again now. "Not bad for a day's work."

I had started work on the CILHI bust. I had to document everything I was doing. That meant stopping frequently to photograph the progress, as well as keeping copious notes, all of which would be turned over to CILHI upon completion of the project.

Dr. Carroway had given me the gender, race and approximate age of the deceased. I could assume nothing about the victim before I began my reconstruct. I pulled the tissue-depth data from one of my charts and carefully measured and cut markers for each part of the face. This was the most painstaking part of the process for me. I worked on it for the bulk of the afternoon, but the fatigue from the trip to Hawaii caught up with me and I turned off the lights and closed the door to my studio at 4:00 p.m. I never close the door to my studio—or any other room in the house—but somehow it seemed like the thing to do this time.

I went in to the kitchen and made myself a cup of hot hibiscus tea. I took my tea back into the living room and sat looking out the French doors at the sights of oncoming spring. I went back in my mind to the first time I met Ted Nikolaides.

I hadn't been in Da Nang for long, when my gregarious friend decided to come and meet the "new girl." He came right into the ward where I worked and introduced himself. He saw I wasn't wearing a wedding band and decided he would find me a man. I laughed at the time at this man so enthusiastic and determined in his old-country matchmaking. It soon became apparent that Ted Nikolaides had a special knack for the task. In the end, Ted had found the perfect man for me—a man who had become the love of my life and with whom I'd had my son. The problem I was having was that my blessings were so numerous and so very much the result of Teddy's friendship and caring. It seemed incredible to me that this reconstruct would be the only way I would finally have to repay such a friend.

I left the living room and went to my bedroom closet. I got a stool and climbed up into the top and pulled down two big boxes. I took them into the living room and set them on the floor. Then I went into the kitchen and brewed more tea.

I brought my tea into the living room and sat down on the floor next to the boxes. I opened the lid on the first one and found in it Jack's badge, his gun and his various citations. I had intended a thousand times to make a special case to display all these things, but somehow I had never gotten around to it.

When Jack had died so suddenly, I had been in shock. I boxed up everything that belonged to him and put it away. It seemed at the time that it was easier to deal with that way. In retrospect, I don't know if it really was or not. I'm not sure anything really makes that kind of separation easier.

I set those things aside and continued to dig in the box. There was a scrapbook I had made of our Vietnam experience. In it were photos of all our friends, the dog we had adopted, the barracks we'd lived in, the dive where we'd eaten and hung out, and Ted. Ted clowning, Ted beaming, Ted laughing. Picture after picture of Ted and Jack yucking it up—the two young bucks in their military uniforms—one a pilot and the other a military policeman.

I felt sick and sad. I could remember meeting Jack—how tall and handsome he was. He was smart and funny, and he had this very sentimental center that he hid from everyone else, but I saw it. Now I could remember the touch of his hand, the feel of his arms and the way he held me. I could remember the smell of his skin—not his cologne, but that wonderful masculine smell that I could only experience when my cheek was right next to his and my nose was pressed against his face.

Time seemed compressed to me now. I didn't feel like a woman of sixty, but the same young girl who had been in Vietnam over thirty years ago. Everything that happened between me and Jack and Ted was yesterday—but it wasn't. Ted had been shot down and now Jack was gone. I sat on the floor with mementos scattered all around me—my past on paper in my hands.

I dropped the scrapbook on the floor in front of me and put my head in my hands, and I wept out loud. "Jack, why couldn't you be here with me now? How could you leave me with this?"

Chapter Eleven

I slept late. I guess the jet lag really got to me. It was 10:00 a.m. and I was still sitting in the kitchen drinking coffee and eating waffles.

I was halfway through the first waffle when Chris Nakis appeared at my front door. I stood before her in an old work shirt with clay stains and holes in it, my shaggiest blue-jean cutoffs and no shoes, with my unwashed hair plastered down to my head. She, on the other hand, was wearing a crisp navy cotton twill skirt and a burgundy cotton short-sleeve shirt and her best sensible shoes. As small and youthful-looking as she appeared for a forty-four-year-old woman, she could have passed that morning for a teenager from one of the local parochial high schools.

I offered her a waffle, but she declined, accepting a cup of my French roast with satisfaction.

"You have news or you wouldn't be here, so what's up?"

"The victim we dug up yesterday morning was a male."

"That's interesting."

"Definitely."

"What's the approximate age of the victim?"

"I'd say somewhere between the ages of thirty and thirty-five."

"It could be Doug Hughes then. The age is right."

"That would explain the similarity between the burial and reburial of the bodies."

"Did you find the same kind of soil samples as before?"

"Well, it looks like it, but I've sent them to A&M again for comparison with the others."

"Did they ever get back to us on the first ones?"

"Not yet, but they've promised me some kind of answer soon."

"I want to start the reconstruct as soon as possible."

"I thought you were working on this CILHI thing."

"I am, but we need some answers in this case. I already know the perpetrator of the crimes against our MIA. I want to get an ID on this Waller Creek victim now."

"Okay, then come on down to the morgue anytime and we'll get started."

"Did you determine yet how this one was killed?"

"It wasn't a bullet to the head. I had to make a thorough inspection of the bones, but I found some marks on the ribs that indicate to me that this person was shot, a couple of times—just not in the head."

"Have you told Leo yet?"

"Actually, she came down to the morgue late yesterday and I went over everything with her."

"Good. I'll be down later today to get started."

I got dressed and went down to my son's office. When I walked into the Homicide Division I was greeted warmly by many old friends. I either knew them because of Jack, or I knew them because of Mike. Either way, they all knew me.

Mike and Tommy were engrossed in some discussion over an open file on Tommy's desk. They both looked up as I approached.

"Hey, Mom. What's up?"

"There's something I want to do, but I don't want to just haul off and do it without clearing it with you two first."

Tommy and Mike looked at each other. They had that "Oh, no" look on their faces.

"I would like to go and talk to Dody Waldrep myself, and I may want to visit with Jimmy Hughes again."

"Mom."

"I'll take Leo with me—unofficially, of course—but I feel the need to talk to Dody in person and to see Jimmy again."

"Mom, you are not investigating this case. You're doing the forensic sculptures, but we are the detectives, and—"

Tommy interrupted. "Why?"

"What?" Mike asked.

"Not you, her—why? Why do you feel you have to talk to him?"

"I want to meet Dody and get a feel for him myself. Then I may want to meet the girl, Lori, too. I want to revisit Jimmy because I feel I could make more progress than I did last time."

"You already made more progress with him than we have," Tommy said. "But here's a news flash for you."

"What?"

"We've had surveillance on him since the second set of bones popped up."

"And?"

"Lori Webster came to his house yesterday, Mom, and she stayed over," Mike added.

Tommy sighed. "We were going to go talk to him, but the truth is, I'm willing to let you try first. He's not going to tell us anything anyway."

"Tommy..." Mike started.

Tommy held up his hand. "Like it or not, Junior, Toni gets more out of this guy."

"What about Dody and Lori?" I asked.

Tommy waved his hand. "Why not? That old drunk seems pretty harmless to me, and the girl is just whacked."

Mike sighed and put his hands on his hips.

"Tommy, you cannot be real. This guy may be drunk, but who knows what he could do, and you're actually going to let my mom go and talk to him?"

"Technically, I can't stop a private citizen from having a conversation with another private citizen. More to the point is the fact that they all might talk more to her than any of them did to you and me, simply because she's a woman and she's not a cop."

"And the risk?" Mike asked.

"Mike, you need to get real. Toni's a black belt in aikido, and if I remember right, she outranks you, pal."

Mike shook his head in frustration.

"Besides, my girlfriend is going with her, and she *is* a cop. She also knows a lot about behavior. I'd like to hear what she thinks about all of them."

"It's our case, Tommy."

"That's ego, man. I'm interested in information. Leo will go with her—off duty." He glared at me.

"Absolutely, off duty," I agreed.

"Leo's a trained law enforcement officer." He picked up his cell phone and dialed. "You'll be fine with her along." He spoke into the cell phone now,

"Hi, talking to Toni here about the two of you going to see Jimmy Hughes again, this Waldrep character, and maybe even the Webster woman..." He paused, so I knew Leo must be talking. "Well, if you'll keep your shirt on five seconds and let me finish, okay? All I was going to say is, they might do more talking to the two of you than they did to us, but you go off duty only, Leo, and wear that ankle holster I gave you like before. No arguments..." He paused again, and then he said goodbye and hung up.

"I'm sure she agreed to those terms," I said.

"She did." He smiled. "Finesse them, Toni. Get me some new information, would you? Right now all I've got is bupkes and two skeletons dug out of the mud."

"I'll do my best."

Leo drove into town from her houseboat on the lake and parked her Jeep in front of my house. I came outside just as she drove up. She got out of the Jeep wearing jeans, a T-shirt and a windbreaker. She pulled up her trouser leg and smiled.

"As ordered," she said.

"I see," I said. "Let's go in my Mustang."

"Cool! I haven't ridden in this hot rod in a while, it'll be fun."

"I think we should visit Jimmy Hughes again first. I want to ask him about Lori Webster and his brother. Let's see if we can get him to tell us any-thing."

"Works for me. Tommy says he's not talking to them. Just stalls them."

I cranked up the Fastback and we backed out of the driveway and took off in a blue streak.

When we got to Jimmy's, he was outside work-ing on his truck in his carport. He pulled his head out from under the hood as we pulled up. He wiped his hands on an old red rag as we walked up the gravel driveway.

"Y'all back again?"

"Hi, Jimmy, how are you?" I asked.

"All right, I guess. Got too many people asking a lot of questions, but other than that, I'm all right."

"I want to ask questions, too, Jimmy. I want to ask questions because I have to know what hap-pened to Addie. Don't you want to know what happened to her?"

He shrugged. "I guess so, although she's gone now and there ain't nothin' I can do about it. Al-ready figured she was gone a long time ago."

"I know you care, Jimmy, because you came for-ward and identified her."

"Way I look at it, I just did what I was supposed to. So, what is it you want to know now?"

He was direct. He definitely did not want us there any longer than necessary. He stood behind the truck and made no move toward the house at all.

"We've been told by your mother that Doug had a girlfriend. A girl named Lori Webster. Do you know her?"

He shrugged again. "I know her. So what?"

"I was wondering if you could tell us anything about their relationship—how involved they might have been. It could make a difference as far as his relationship with Addie."

"He dated Lori, and I already told you that I know he and Addie didn't have a thing. What else?"

"I was hoping you could give us more details than that, Jimmy."

"Like what?"

"How involved he might have really been with Lori, and anything you know about her now."

"Can't help you."

That was it. He shifted from one foot to the other, and rolled some of the gravel from the driveway under his right boot.

"That all?" he asked.

I sighed. He wasn't giving, and we knew from Mike and Tommy that Lori had just been here the day before. He was a tough case. He had seen too many things in the war, and he just wanted to be left alone. I knew too many men from my generation who were just like him.

"I got to finish working on my truck."

I could see he wasn't going to talk today, so we said our goodbyes and left Jimmy Hughes to finish his truck maintenance.

We drove out to Manor. It was an icky day weatherwise. It wasn't really overcast, but it wasn't sunny either. It was one of those depressing low-light days where the sun comes and goes and you wish it would just do one or the other and stay that way. We talked about the case on the way to Manor.

"What did you think about Jimmy?" I asked.

"He does a great imitation of a clam."

I nodded. "The problem is, I can't tell if he's really hiding something, or he's just being him."

"I watched his eye movements while you were talking to him. His eyes shift to the left a lot, and he looks down. He also exhibits other minute body-language cues, especially the way he blinks and his eyebrow movements—all these cues that I noticed are cues for evasion and lying."

"So, he *is* hiding something."

She nodded. "I believe he is. You know the stats on who discovers the body, right?"

"You mean, the person to discover the body is usually the killer—those stats?"

"Right. The same stats would apply to someone who ID's a body."

"Like what Jimmy did."

"Exactly like what he did. It could be a coincidence that he saw Addie's face on the news and that he was the first one to call in, but the stats say it probably isn't."

"He was never involved with her, and he hadn't seen her in over twenty years, so why was he so interested in identifying her?" I mused out loud.

"He had a potential motive, and he's been seen recently with someone else who had a similar motive."

"Lori Webster."

"Lori Webster," she affirmed. "Think about it, Toni, either one of them could have done this alone, or they could have done it together. Why would these two people—one who moved away to Austin almost thirty years ago, and one who moved to Georgetown sixteen years ago—why would these two people still have anything to do with each other? They have one thing in common as far as I can see."

"He loved Addie, and she loved Doug."

"Bingo."

"Jimmy had been left behind years ago, but gave up when Addie married Dody, then he finds out his brother is having a thing with Addie—and at the same time Lori is getting dumped off by Doug."

"It'll be interesting to talk to Dody in person—to get his take on all this. Jimmy says his brother wasn't involved with Addie. I wonder what Dody says."

"Apparently he's not saying much of anything to the boys."

I pulled off the main road and drove up the gravel driveway to the front of Dody's ramshackle little house. It looked virtually abandoned. There was an old, beat-up, partially rusted-out pickup truck parked to the left side of the house. In the front yard, a chicken wandered by, and out in the grass amongst the cedar trees two goats grazed.

"Lovely," Leo remarked.

"What did you expect for a guy who's drunk ninety percent of the time? He hasn't held a job for more than six months in the last fourteen years."

"Great."

We walked up onto the rickety wooden porch and I knocked on the door. Dody answered. He was wearing worn and dirty jeans and a filthy white T-shirt that had a hole in the left sleeve and one in the bottom near the hem. He reeked of everything foul.

He cleared his throat. "I ain't buyin' nothin' today, ladies," and he started to close the door.

"I'm not selling anything, Mr. Waldrep. I'm the forensic sculptor who reconstructed the face of your wife. This other lady is an associate of mine."

He stopped his closure of the door and squinted at both of us. "What do you want with me? I already talked to them cops. I don't know nothin' about what happened to my wife. I don't have nothin' else to say about it."

"Please, Mr. Waldrep. We just have a couple of questions and then we'll go."

He continued squinting at Leo and me, and then opened the door. "Come on in then, but don't tarry too long. I got things to do."

I doubted that seriously. The only thing I imagined that Dody Waldrep had to do was to drink more than he already had. He was slurring his words, and as we watched him walk through the room back to his chair, we exchanged glances that told me Leo had also noticed the wobble in his step.

He practically fell into the chair, and then motioned for Leo and me to sit on the sofa. It was a horrible excuse for furniture and I imagined that it was probably a breeding ground for all manner of mites and who knew what else, but I sat anyway.

"So, what is it you need to know that I ain't already been asked?"

"First of all, Mr. Waldrep, are you aware that more bones were found near the river yesterday?"

"Heard sumpthin' about it on the news. Didn't pay much attention."

"You didn't think that it sounded familiar to the way in which your wife's bones were found?"

"Didn't think about it. She's been found, we buried her, end of story."

"It didn't occur to you that these might be the bones of Doug Hughes?"

"Huh," he grunted. "Who in blazes cares?"

"Mr. Waldrep, don't you wonder what happened to them after they left Viola."

"I don't have no reason to wonder. I know what they done, and I don't care what kind of trouble they run into. Whatever it was, it'd serve 'em right I say."

"Then you do believe that Addie and Doug were having an affair?"

"I don't believe it—I know it."

"How do you know, Mr. Waldrep?"

"I know, that's all. I was her husband, you know. You people are incredible. You think I lived with her and I don't know," he snorted, and then wiped his nose on his sleeve.

"Do you have any idea who might have wanted to kill Addie and Doug?"

"Well, it wasn't me, that's all I say. They run off before I had any kind of opportunity for that, and I was too busy trying to make ends meet and all after they left."

"So, then, you don't have any idea who it could have been?"

"What did I just say, lady? Isn't that what I just said?"

"Well, I guess I just thought you might want some of these questions answered yourself."

"I don't have no questions, lady. My wife run off with him, she's dead now and buried. There ain't no more questions as far as I'm concerned. Got it?"

Leo looked at me and nodded. We had indeed "gotten it" and we said our goodbyes to Dody and left.

Once we were safely back in my car, we talked about our brief encounter with Dody.

"Tommy won't be happy with me, since I learned nothing new from either Jimmy or Dody," I said.

"We did learn something new, though."

"What?"

"We learned that Jimmy is definitely hiding something, and we learned that Addie's husband believed that she was having an affair with Doug. So, one of them is right and the other is wrong, but they've both given us some interesting things to think about."

"You think he could have killed them?"

"Dody?"

I nodded.

"He could have. He's pretty disorganized, though. I don't see him planning everything the way it would have been planned originally. He's the right personality for the dumping of these bodies, though."

"What if he wasn't this messed up back then?" I asked.

"Didn't that lady at the diner say he always had problems?"

"She said he was cantankerous," I said, "but she didn't say when specifically he began having a drinking problem. His daughters didn't go live with their grandmother until two years after their mother disappeared."

"Well, I suppose if he were less impaired by the alcohol sixteen years ago, he might have been capable of the crime, but it's really impossible now to know."

"Let's pay a visit to Lori Webster," I suggested, "and see what we can find there."

"Okay. I'm game if you are."

We sped up the highway to Georgetown and I wheeled the car into the town square, scoping for a spot in front of the store where she worked. We found a space just around the corner, and I parked the car.

Once inside the store, we asked for Lori and we were directed up to the office. There we introduced ourselves to her, and she led us into a small room off the main office. The room contained a copier, a fax machine and several file cabinets. Lori wore a dark green skirt and white blouse with a beige cardigan over it. She was a frail-looking woman, with stringy shoulder-length brown hair. I think her eyes were gray, but from the moment we met her, she never looked us in the eye. It was just as Mike and Tommy had said.

"You said you're the artist who reconstructed Addie's face?"

She fidgeted with her hands, fluttering her eyelids when she spoke and punctuating her phrases with frustrated sighs.

"Yes, that's right."

"So, what can I do for you?"

"Well, we found similar remains in another location in Austin the other day, and it's been determined that they are the remains of a man."

She looked up from her hands and looked upward. "Doug? Is it Doug?"

She still didn't look at either one of us. Her eyes shot to the right wall. She was as strange as the boys had said.

"We don't know yet. I'll be doing the reconstruct, just as I did with Mrs. Waldrep. I mostly just wanted to let you know what was happening, and to see if there was anything else you think of that you hadn't told the officers the other day."

She sat for a while. She was looking at her hands again. She was becoming more emotional now. She began to cry. I reached into my purse and pulled out a tissue and handed it to her. She mopped up her tears with the tissue.

"I don't know anything more than what I said the other day. He just disappeared and that's all I know."

She was sobbing now and I tried to comfort her, but she pulled away. She regained control of herself somewhat, and I decided to try for another question.

"Ms. Webster, do you know Doug's brother Jimmy?"

"Of course," she said. "He's been a good friend to me."

"You've seen him recently, then?"

She hesitated and became more nervous. She seemed confused. She looked down at the wadded-up tissue she held in her hands.

She hesitated a second and then said distantly, "He takes care of me. He helps me with things."

"Like what things?"

She wadded the tissue into twists and knots.

"Just things," she said. "I don't think I feel very good now. I don't want to talk anymore."

Leo and I looked at each other, and Leo nodded.

"All right, Ms. Webster, I guess we'll go."

"When will you know if it's Doug?"

She still looked down at the tissue.

"It will be several days, but I'll ask the detectives to contact you and let you know."

She nodded but didn't look up.

We excused ourselves and left her sitting there fidgeting.

"Very strange girl," I said when we got back in the car.

"That's the understatement of the century," Leo said.

"So, what's your appraisal?"

"She has a serious mental problem. I don't think she's completely in touch with reality, and she has a kind of childlike or withdrawn nature. She even seemed to be drifting in and out of her grip when we were talking to her. If she's had declining mental health all this time, she could have committed the crimes back then, and now she definitely fits as the kind of person who would carry out this disorganized and illogical reburial situation."

"She acted genuinely surprised about us finding the second set of bones."

"Maybe she is," Leo said, "or maybe she's so delusional it did surprise her."

"Think Jimmy helped her?"

"I think he could have helped her, and that could be what she was talking about, or he knows what she did and he's covering for her, or the other way around even."

"Think there's any possibility that Addie and Doug did run off, and someone else killed them?"

"Anything's possible, Toni. I want to see the face on those bones we just found."

"I'll start on it as soon as we get back."

"The guy we found yesterday had been shot multiple times, and it wasn't in the head. In fact, the bullets scraped and bounced off his ribs."

"So what does that mean to you?"

"It means whoever he was, he wasn't executed like Addie. It means this guy was killed in haste and that wasn't part of the killer's plan."

"That might fit if Lori were the killer. You know, she killed Doug in a rage, then executed Addie."

"It'd be the other way around, the way I see it. She executed Addie, Doug caught her, so she killed him in haste—may have even regretted it instantly."

"That could be the source of her reality gap."

"It would also explain dumping Addie's bones on Red Bud, while burying Doug to be discovered up on the trail."

"I'll do my work, and then we'll see for sure if this is Doug Hughes that we've found."

I had worked two days on this bust already. The first day, I had done all the grueling work of measuring, cutting and applying all the tissue-depth indicators, until the skull had the full "eraser measles." Then I had tediously applied the clay across all the markers. Now I sat on my high stool in front of the workbench with a cup of hot hibiscus tea in my hands and looked at the almost completed work. I only had to finish and smooth a few areas and it would be done.

The head of this man was broad and round, the cheekbones big and high. The brow was low, but not particularly pronounced and the nose was like an upside-down anvil, with a strong long line down the middle, but with the sides flaring out at the nostrils. The lips were thick and the mouth large. It was a handsome face, but not in a pretty-boy way. It was a rugged face. Now the question would be, was it Doug Hughes's face?

⚘ Chapter Twelve ⚘

One month earlier, on all local channels, the plea of a mother had been broadcast. Her name was Nadine Ferguson and her son had been missing for over sixteen years. The day of the broadcast had been his birthday. Mrs. Ferguson, now a widow, was seriously ill and dying of cancer. She only wanted to see her son one last time, or at least to know what had happened to him. Mrs. Ferguson lived in Houston, but her son had lived in Hempstead at the time of his disappearance. He was a good boy, she had said. He loved his simple life in Hempstead, working in a local clothing store as a salesman, walking and hiking in the local area observing and sketching birds. He hadn't an enemy in the world and, in fact, everyone in Hempstead who knew him loved to be around him.

Brian Ferguson was thirty years old at the time of his disappearance from Hempstead. Now we knew that he was thirty years old at the time of his death. I had worked for three solid days to get the image out and get it right. Mike and Tommy knew as soon as I was done with it that it wasn't Doug Hughes. I didn't want to see his photo, in case I ever had to do another reconstruct that might be him. Tommy and Mike had pulled his Texas driver's-license photo and compared it to my bust.

"It's not him, Mom."

I couldn't believe it when Mike told me.

"That can't be right."

"It can and it is. It's just not him, Mom."

"Then who in blazes is it?"

"Don't know, but we're broadcasting the image and releasing it to all the papers."

The image was only broadcast once when Mrs. Ferguson called in to the number on the screen to tell Tommy Lucero that the image on the bust was the face of her son. His Texas driver's-license photo was pulled and compared. It was a match. His mother provided dental records for comparison and the forensic dentist in Chris's office reviewed them. They were a match also. The bones belonged to Brian Ferguson.

As soon as I got the news, I called Leo.

"Guess Tommy told you, it's not Doug Hughes. So, now what do you think?" I asked.

"I think we have a whole new mystery on our hands. I think we need to find out if there is any connection between Addie and this guy, Brian Ferguson."

"What about Doug Hughes? Do you think any of this could have anything to do with why Doug is still missing?"

"Who knows? Until we find him, we won't know. Tommy said Brian's mother had put out some kind of plea for information on television about a month ago, right?"

"Yes."

"No matter who the killer is, that was the trigger, Toni."

"What do you mean?"

"That's what I've been looking for. It's like I said about the type of wounds that killed Brian, and where he was reburied. Killing Brian wasn't part of his plan."

"Okay."

"The killer saw Mrs. Ferguson on TV and it probably made him feel bad. I think digging up Brian and reburying him where someone would find him— that was the purpose I was talking about."

"So, it was guilt?"

"Yeah. That was all about giving Mrs. Ferguson the answer to her plea, and assuaging the killer's guilt over killing Brian. Brian was a mistake that had to be corrected. The killer had probably buried them in the same place originally. So he digs up Brian to rebury him where he can be found—for Mrs. Ferguson—but he digs up Addie in the process and decides to get rid of her while he's at it. It could have been Jimmy, or Lori, or Dody, or maybe even Doug himself."

"Dody seemed to be so sure Addie and Doug were involved," I said. "Maybe they were, maybe this Brian guy came along and messed things up and Doug is the killer."

"We definitely need to find Doug Hughes."

"Yes, and I need to find out more about Brian Ferguson. I need to try to find out how he's connected to Addie and Doug."

Brian's funeral had been well attended by Mrs. Ferguson, her friends and all of the people in Hempstead who had known and worked with Brian. He had been a very popular guy. Ironically, the one enemy he had, had been no one he knew at all as far as any of us could tell. My only consolation in his sad death was in knowing that my work had answered the questions of a grief-stricken and dying mother.

I was back at work on the CILHI case again, trying to answer the questions of a grief-stricken widow—my friend Irini. The answer to this question might bring closure to her and her children. The clay was going on, but slowly. I was totally preoccupied with the other case—or maybe it just provided me with a convenient excuse to avoid the CILHI work.

I had been sure that the bones found at Waller Creek would be those of Doug Hughes. Doug was still missing, and now I was wondering what had happened to him.

I stopped my work on the CILHI bust and decided to make tea and think about what I wanted for lunch. About that time, the phone rang and it was Chris. She asked me to meet her and Leo for lunch. She had some news for us. I changed out of my old jeans and clay-stained work shirt and put on some nice black slacks, a plum-colored, short-sleeve knit top and some comfortable black sandals. It was an awesome day outside, so I rode with the windows down and the breeze in my hair.

I was to meet Chris and Leo at Gordon's Lakeside out on Lake Travis, so I headed from my part of town in Hyde Park and took the winding Bull Creek Road out to the lake highway. I loved to drive the curves on Bull Creek in the Fastback. It gave me a chance to really go through the gears and feel the wheel. Once I went under the loop, I opened up that little Pony. On the segment of Bull Creek from the loop to the lake road there were few curves, but there was more opportunity to blow some soot out of the cylinders, as my dad liked to say. There was also one very large hill at one point, and if you got up a good head of steam, you could plow that hill from bottom to top in fourth gear, and that's exactly what I did.

The wind was really blowing through the cockpit of my little land jet, and it felt good. I made a left turn onto the lake highway and headed toward Mansfield Dam, the big dam that created Lake Travis. I took the highway across the river, just below the dam, and once on the other side, I made a right turn down a narrow county road, then off the beaten path down a dirt road and into the parking lot of Gordon's. The place was surrounded by trees and then it opened up onto the lakeshore.

Susan Gordon was an old friend of Leo's and ran the place. At night, there was live music out on the deck with a breathtaking view of the water. The deck was almost at lake level, and you could come to Gordon's by boat and dock at the far end. People packed Susan's place for lunch, dinner and late-night snacks. It was a local favorite, and definitely one of my favorites because of the lake view.

We sat outdoors. The daytime chill was giving way to more moderate spring temperatures, and the Texas sun was unencumbered that day. We had all ordered our food and the iced tea had been delivered to the table, when Chris broke the news.

"I got the soil sample results back from A&M. They say that both sets of bones contain soil samples that are exact matches."

"And the location?" I asked.

"One set of soil samples is from this area, and the other soil shows composition similar to soils that would be found in and around Hempstead."

"Where Brian Ferguson was living at the time of his death," I said.

"Exactly," Chris responded.

"Then Addie Waldrep and Brian Ferguson were buried in that area, which means it's probably where they were both killed," Leo said.

"The burning question now is, what was Addie doing down near Hempstead with Brian Ferguson?" I asked.

"Yeah, and where is Doug Hughes?" Chris asked.

"Well, if he's still alive, who knows where he is or how to find him, but..." Leo trailed off.

"If he's dead, he's probably buried in Hempstead?" Chris asked.

"Or, he could be reburied somewhere here," I said.

"I'd say it's fifty-fifty," Leo agreed. "If the killer dug them all up trying to get to Brian, and then reburied Addie, he might have done the same with Doug, if Doug is dead."

"But we haven't found any more bones," Chris said.

"Not yet," I offered. "And if the killer intended them to wash away like Addie's, then we may never find them."

"He might have even reburied them on Red Bud and they already washed away," Leo said.

Chris shook her head. "There was no evidence of that at that site, but he could have reburied them nearby."

"If the chance is fifty-fifty, then I'd say our chances are better in Hempstead," I said.

"How do you figure that?" Leo asked.

"No matter where any of them were reburied, there *is* an original burial site probably in Hempstead."

"True," Leo agreed.

"How accurate are the soil samples from A&M?" I asked.

"Accurate? Depends on what you mean by that. If you mean will they swear by their results, then they will," Chris said.

"I guess what I really mean is how close can you narrow it down to the exact site."

"You can't do that, Toni," Chris said. "They're accurate as to the part of Texas, even to a reasonably small region, like the area around Hempstead, but that's all."

"Then we couldn't possibly use the sample to narrow our search for the burial site."

"No. You still have hundreds of acres or more to consider based on this soil sample, and that's as 'accurate' as it will ever get. Well, unless we knew the site, and we could take a sample from it and do a comparison."

"If we can find the site, we could probably literally dig up more evidence—more clues. Is that what you're thinking?" Leo asked.

I nodded, sighed and ran my fingers through my hair. Then something occurred to me.

"Maybe we don't need soil samples to narrow the search."

"What do you mean?" Leo said expectantly.

"The site might be one where Brian liked to go. You know, a place he would take someone like Addie."

"He lived there, Toni. His mother told Tommy and Mike he hiked all over that area bird-watching. It could be anywhere."

"Not necessarily. Bird-watchers usually go to specific places looking for specific species. Besides, I remember Mike and Tommy telling me that Brian did his bird-watching with some of his local friends. If he had particular places he liked to go to see certain birds, they would know. His mother might even know, if we asked that question."

"You're going to go talk to his mother, aren't you?" Leo asked.

"Well, I think I need to talk to Brian's mother, and maybe even some of the good people of Hempstead. I think I can start with Mrs. Ferguson and find out what she knows, and if she can tell me who Brian's good friends were. Then I can look them up and have a chat with them."

"Mike and Tommy will love that," Chris said, rolling her eyes.

Leo snickered. "They gave us permission before."

"I want to do this on my own this time, Leo. I've been wanting to talk to Mrs. Ferguson anyway. I'll ask Mike and Tommy before I do anything, but I really did wish I could sit down and have a woman-to-woman talk with Mrs. Ferguson. You know, one widow to another, one mother to another. This would be a good opportunity for that."

I smiled and raised my eyebrows. Chris and Leo just shook their heads and smiled back. About that time, lunch was brought to the table and we dug in.

After lunch was over, I decided I needed another drive to Viola. I had a couple of questions for my new friend Doris. I wanted more information on any possible connection between Addie and Brian before I went to Houston to talk to Mrs. Ferguson.

The drive took about an hour. I hadn't had dessert after my lunch with Chris and Leo, and all I could think of was Doris's awesome apple pie. I hoped there was some left after her lunch crowd.

I pulled off the interstate and headed up the county road that led to Viola. I turned off on the main road that was downtown Viola. I pulled up in front of the café, easily finding a parking spot. The lunch crowd had dissipated, so I knew that Doris would have some time to spend with me. I hopped out of the Mustang and strode to the front door, and was greeted heartily by Doris. I assumed my usual spot at the lunch counter. Doris was already dishing up my pie.

Doris slid my slab of apple pie across the counter and winked. "There you go, hon."

"Ah, the famous pie." I smacked my lips as I picked up my fork.

"Well, I haven't ever had someone drive over sixty miles for my pie."

"Well, you have now."

"Darlin', I know my pie is good, but it ain't that good. You've got more questions for old Doris, don't you?"

I chuckled. She was a sweet, country-café proprietor who smelled like everyone's grandma—and she had a mind sharp as a razor blade.

"Well, Doris, I do have a question or two, but I salivated over this pie all the way here. I could have just called you with my questions, you know." I smiled as I shoveled in another mouthwatering piece.

"True." Doris smiled back as she made a loud pop on her chewing gum. "Well, then, I guess questions or no, my pie does have some drawing power after all."

"Absolutely."

"Well, hon, what is it you wanted to know?"

"I guess you heard on the news about the second body found."

"Oh yes. I heard. Some young man from Houston?"

"That's right. We think he was killed by accident, but I just want to make sure that he wasn't someone Addie knew, or someone who had ever been seen around here."

"What was the boy's name again?"

"Brian Ferguson."

Doris pursed her lips and then shook her head, "No, hon, that just don't sound familiar at all. Do you have a picture of him? I saw it on TV the other night, but I wasn't looking that close and I've slept a few times since then." She smacked and then popped her gum.

I did have Brian's picture with me. It was a copy of the Texas driver's-license photo that Chris had given me. I pulled the picture out of my wallet and handed it over to Doris.

Doris scrutinized it carefully and then pronounced, "Nope. I've absolutely never seen this young man."

"You're sure."

"I see everyone who ever comes to this town— distant relatives from out of town, old school chums, new love interests, you name it, hon, old Doris hears and sees it all."

At least Doris had never seen him, and didn't know of a connection between him and Addie, but I wasn't about to give up. I would talk to his mother, and his friends in Hempstead. Maybe someone would have a clue.

"Well, Doris, as usual you've been a great help. The pie was as awesome as ever."

"I'm just glad that you love my pie that much." She smiled and popped her gum one more time.

I paid for my pie and got back into my car. I had found out part of what I wanted to know and had gotten a really good dessert out of the trip.

On the way back to Austin, my cell phone rang. It was Drew.

"Toni, I want your update on this bone case of yours, and the young man from Hempstead, plus I have something special for you. Can you come by?"

"Absolutely. I'm on my way back into town, and I can probably be at your office in about forty-five minutes."

"Sounds great. I'll brew us some Earl Grey."

I chuckled at the thought of all those hard-core Texas Rangers sucking down rot-gut coffee out at Ranger headquarters, and Drew in his office with his cup of Earl Grey. He was one in a million. I was glad he had called. I wanted to tell Drew more about the Red Bud case. I didn't just want his opinion. I thought we might need his help outside of the Austin jurisdiction. If I was right about finding the original burial site, then Drew could be of help with local law enforcement.

I wheeled into the parking lot at Ranger headquarters and went up to Drew's office. When I got there, he was on the phone and motioned for me to come in and sit down, so I seated myself in a chair in front of his desk.

Drew finished his call, and said, "Toni, I'm glad you could make it by."

"So am I."

He served me my tea and then smiled and gave me a sly look out of the corner of his eye as he went back around the desk, and pulled out a small package of Walker shortbread.

I shook my head. "Drew Smith, you sly dog..." I couldn't bear to tell him I just ate pie an hour ago. Drew knew that I loved Walker shortbread.

He laughed. "Now, Toni, I'm a gentleman. You don't think I'd invite a lady to my office and not offer her proper refreshments."

"You're the limit, Drew."

"Well, not exactly. That tea was prepared in the microwave down the hall." He smiled again.

I was already sipping my tea. "It's wonderful—microwave or not."

"Well, good," he said, satisfied with his efforts. "So, tell me, Dr. Antoinette, how are you today?"

I winced at the use of my full name.

"You know, I'd appreciate it if you stuck with my nicknames—particularly in public."

He chuckled mischievously. "I just love to push your buttons, Toni."

I shook my head again.

"So, what's happening with your Red Bud bones case?"

"I'm sure you saw in the papers where another set of bones had been discovered."

"Yes, and linked to some guy from Houston? I've also heard rumblings about Hempstead and a burial site out of town—which means the murder probably did not occur in Austin."

"Probably didn't. Chris says the A&M has matched the soil samples to the same kind of soil in and around Hempstead, which is where the latest victim was living."

"Brian Ferguson?"

"Right. That same soil was found in the bones of Addie Waldrep. So they were previously buried in that area."

"Which means they were probably murdered in that area."

"Which means you're thinking about jurisdiction."

"Mmm, hmm. Tell me what you know so far."

I told him all about what we knew about Addie Waldrep, Jimmy Hughes, Dody Waldrep and Lori Webster. I told him that Doug Hughes was still missing. I told him I was going to go and visit Mrs. Ferguson and see what I could find out.

"I just came back from the Viola area, where the first victim lived. I questioned someone up there about any connection between Addie Waldrep and Brian Ferguson, but I struck out."

"Why is it I think you're not giving up on that angle?" He smiled.

"Because you know me too well."

"I think you're on the right path talking to the young man's mother. I'd like you to pursue that. If you can isolate some places he normally went bird-watching, maybe we can get some warrants and do some searching. But we can't search the whole county down there."

"I know. Maybe I can eliminate some places you won't have to search. So, are you going to get officially involved?"

"I want to see what you come up with first. Then I'll need to talk to Tommy and Mike. If this thing really looks like something that involves multiple jurisdictions, I'll call them and we can talk about it."

"You won't be calling them until I come back from Houston, then."

"No, Toni. I have my hands full right now."

"Good."

"And I want you to let me know exactly what you find out on your trip to Houston."

"You got it."

❦ Chapter Thirteen ❦

After meeting with Drew, I had called Michael and arranged to meet him at our dojo for an aikido workout. My son and I were both black belts in the art, although at different levels—I had begun teaching him when he was nine—and we both served as instructors there as much as our schedules would allow. Lately, my schedule hadn't even allowed for much in the way of workouts.

Mike met me there and the two of us sparred with a group of black belts who regularly met there on Tuesday evenings. I was rusty and needed the workout badly. My son almost beat me, but the old lady was still ahead and I proved I could teach him a few things.

When we were done with the workout, we cleaned up and buzzed over to one of our favorite Tex-Mex joints to meet Tommy. He was crunching on tostadas and gulping down gallons of tea when we arrived.

Mike and I ordered water and tea, too.

The waiter brought our beverages, and we ordered our food. "So, who won the big sparring match tonight?" Tommy asked.

Mike cleared his throat, and gave Tommy the corner eye shot that silently told him, "Don't go there, man."

Tommy started to chuckle. "I love it, she kicked your rear again." He laughed out loud now.

Mike sighed, shook his head and put his hand over his eyes.

"Well, I was his teacher, Tommy, and I do outrank him. Besides, he was doing really well at first. It took me a while to get a handle on him tonight."

"Hey, man, don't feel bad," Tommy said to Mike. "My mom kicks my rear every time I go home and she's not even into martial arts. She's a little stick of dynamite."

We all laughed now. I knew Mrs. Lucero, and I could just imagine her keeping Tommy right in line.

"So, Tommy, when are you going to come to the dojo and start taking lessons?" Mike said.

"Are you interested in aikido?" I asked.

"Well," Tommy said, "I've seen Junior here get some suspects under control in real short order and without a lot of energy expense. So, I just thought it might be a good idea to at least explore the merits, you know, see what it's like."

"He's chicken," Mike said.

"Whoa, partner! I am not chicken. I just don't want you to be my teacher, that's all. I got to put up with you all day long, I don't want to have to put up with you in the dojo, too."

"We have a lot of great teachers, Tommy," I said, "but you know you do have to show deference to all the black belts."

"That's okay. I understand that, but I would prefer to learn from you, Toni."

I smiled. "Let me know when you're ready and I'll be happy to teach you."

The food was delivered to the table and there wasn't a lot of chatter while the boys wolfed down their dinner as if they hadn't eaten in three days. I thought with their mouths full, it would be a good time for me to update them on what I had learned recently, and the latest thoughts I had about the case. I filled them in and they listened without much comment.

"So, what I'd like to do now—with your blessing, of course—is go visit Mrs. Ferguson. I'd like to talk to her about Brian's habits, but I'd also like to just visit with her a little. This whole case, and the way Brian was killed in particular, really gets to me, and as one mother to another, I'd like to visit with her."

"Mom, I just don't think that's a good idea. I mean, you've been to see Jimmy, Dody and Lori, and you didn't really find out anything new, so I don't see the point."

"We did find out something new. We found out Jimmy is withholding something."

"Leo thinks," Mike said.

"We also know that Jimmy wants us to believe that Addie and Doug were not involved with one another, but that Dody believes they definitely were. That could become important later."

"Mom, we don't need civilians poking around in all this. We can close the case on our own."

"Excuse me, but I'd like to point out a few things here," Tommy interjected. "First of all, don't talk to your mom like that. It's rude, and it bothers me—a lot."

Mike sighed.

"Hey, this ain't the dojo, man. I'm the senior guy here. You may not like it, Mike, but your mom is not a civilian. She's in law enforcement—she's a forensic artist and scientist. You don't have to carry a badge and a gun to be in law enforcement. My sister is a toxicologist at the State Crime Lab. She's in law enforcement, too."

"Yeah, but your sister doesn't go all over the place questioning people."

"That's only because she's a science geek and that isn't her thing. Your mother is good at this and people talk to her. She might have gotten something out of Dody, but as it is, she didn't hurt anything by talking to him either—and it did help us to have Leo observe him, and Jimmy and Lori, and give us her assessment."

"Thank you, Tommy," I said.

"Toni put the faces back on both of these victims, Mike. Frankly, I don't know how she does that without getting involved with them. I think it would mess me up. It doesn't surprise me that she has to know." Tommy turned to me now. "There's no harm, Toni, in you talking to Mrs. Ferguson. I'll give you her number. She's not dangerous and she's not a suspect. You're both widows and mothers of a son. She may very well remember things in talking to you that she didn't when she talked to me and Mike. Plus, she was really touched by what you did for her. Might be good for her to get to meet you. I feel sorry for her, too. She doesn't have long to live, and she didn't deserve for any of this horror to happen to her."

His eyes misted up a little now. He was fiery sometimes, but Tommy Lucero had that sentimental heart. Sometimes it served him well, as in this case. Sometimes it burdened him with guilt, as with the death of Bobby Driskill.

"I never thought about it that way," Mike said. "I'm sorry, Mom. I was wrong to jump all over you. I just didn't think about all that stuff."

"That's because you got your ego wrapped so tight around your head, it's like a tourniquet on your brain," Tommy said.

I busted out laughing. Then Tommy started to laugh and Mike couldn't help but join in.

When our laughter tapered off, Tommy said, "Okay, just one thing, Toni."

"What's that?"

"You share whatever you find down there."

"That's a given, Tomas. That's always a given."

I had called Mrs. Ferguson and told her I was the artist who had done the bust of her son. She was glad to speak with me and thanked me for what I had done for her. I told her I appreciated her comments, but that finding Brian's remains was luck, and someone else's "luck" at that—all I had done was my job. When I told her that I would like to come down and visit with her, she readily agreed.

The weather the next morning was grim. It was gray and cloudy and it drizzled all morning. It didn't improve any as I got closer to Houston. I followed Mrs. Ferguson's directions and arrived at her home about 10:30 a.m. I had dressed in my nicest black slacks, a dark green cotton shirt with three-quarter-length sleeves and my "citified" short, black zip-up boots. I pulled up to the curb in my black Pony and shut the power plant off to hear the soft pattering of rainfall on the roof and windshield. I grabbed a slicker from the back seat, threw it on over my clothes and exited the car.

Down the street about three houses away, I could have sworn that I saw Lori Webster. It was gray and rainy and difficult to see. I went toward the person, but she turned and hurried away from me. I wasn't going to chase her in the rain. It certainly looked like her, but I couldn't be a hundred percent sure. If it was her, I wondered why on earth she would come here to Mrs. Ferguson's.

As I got to the front door, Mrs. Ferguson opened it. She must have heard the rumble of the Mustang pulling up out front. She was thin and her hand quivered slightly as she extended it to me. I could see the blue veins through her delicate skin, but the brightness was there in her eyes. I could see her spirit had not dimmed in spite of all the tragedy she had endured.

"Toni?" she said.

"Yes, ma'am."

"Come in. I have coffee for us."

She had a nice little house in a middle-class suburb in Houston. The house was a light-colored brick, single-story home with off-white trim and shutters. It was about two thousand square feet and as neat and tidy inside as any home I'd ever seen. We sat in her sunroom and had our coffee and just chatted for a few minutes.

"Well, Toni, it's so nice to meet you after what you've done for me, but I know you didn't come here just to socialize. You have something to discuss with me about Brian, I'm sure."

"Yes, Mrs. Ferguson, I do. My son is one of the homicide detectives on the case..."

"I wondered if the name Sullivan for both of you was a coincidence or not."

"No, ma'am, it isn't."

"He was such a nice boy. Actually, both of the detectives were kind to me. Your son seems like such a nice man, though."

"Thank you, Mrs. Ferguson."

"Oh, you must call me Nadine. I'm sorry, Toni, you were trying to tell me something about the case?"

"Yes, Nadine. I was saying that I'm working with the police to try to put some things together about this case. We have one investigator working with us who has helped us develop some behavioral theories. In connection with that, and trying to gather more evidence to help bring it all together, I was hoping you could give me some idea of where Brian liked to go to do his hiking and bird watching, and maybe tell me something about his friends in Hempstead."

"Oh. Oh, dear. Well, he mentioned several places. I'm not sure if I can remember the names, though. Let me see.... Oh, it's been so long."

"Well, if you can't remember the places, maybe you remember some of the people who knew him in Hempstead. People that might know where he did his bird watching."

"You know, I know I can do that. He had two very good friends at that time, both of whom even occasionally went with him. They would know where he went."

"Good."

"Let's see, the one he had his eye on was a girl named Julie Paine, and her friend was a girl named Frances Miller."

"Do you know if they both still live in Hempstead?"

"Yes, they do. They were both at Brian's funeral. Frances is married and has two children now. Poor little Julie never married, and appears to be quite grief-stricken over Brian even still. They were all very good friends then."

"This is very helpful, Nadine. They may be able to give us the kind of information we need."

"Yes, they would know better than me really."

We sat quietly for a few seconds.

"You know," Nadine said, "the man Brian worked for in Hempstead might be able to help you also. He still runs that same clothing store. It's called Wolfram's and it's in the town square. He knew Brian really well."

"Oh, that could be helpful, too."

"Toni, why don't we go look at some of Brian's sketches. You're an artist, and I'm very proud of his work. I'd like you to see them."

"I would love that."

We got up and went down the hall to a little room with windows all across one wall. It looked like a study, and with all the windows, it was light even on a gloomy day like that one. The study had become a gallery to Brian's work. She showed me framed drawings of birds in the wild from all sorts of places. Apparently, Brian would travel to other locations from time to time to study and sketch the birds. The bookshelves were filled with books on ornithology. Suddenly, I noticed one book on the shelf that had the name Ferguson on the spine.

"Oh, what is this?"

"That was Brian's book. He had a doctorate in ornithology."

"I had no idea. That explains the bird watching."

"Yes, but as you can see, he was a really good artist."

"Yes, he really was. His work is very nice."

"He just wanted to focus on his art and the birds without the pressure of a high-stress job. It was what he loved."

Nadine and I talked for a while longer. As a mother, I couldn't imagine what she had been through and was still going through now. Her husband had died two years ago and we discussed things that only a widow could understand. I thought about this brave woman, carrying on with what was left of her life. She told me that she only had about four months left, according to her doctors. She was enjoying what she had as much as possible, but she was ready, she said, to go to the other side. She said her life was richer now in understanding how precious each moment was. She had a close network of friends and she was maximizing her time with them. I felt better in hearing that, but sad still that this sweet woman was not someone I would have time to know better.

We brought our conversation to a close, I thanked Nadine for the coffee and made up my mind to go to Hempstead on my way back to Austin. Hempstead was only about an hour out of Houston and not really far off the beaten path back to my city. I didn't know how wild Mike would be about the idea, but I wasn't some little schoolgirl, and I thought Tommy wouldn't object. I was going to do it anyway, because I needed the answers myself. Besides, I was saving them some footwork and they had other cases to work on. That one sounded really good in my head when I came up with it anyway.

As you drive up the coastal plain from Houston toward Hempstead, you move into the beautiful, lush green forests and hidden piney woods of Texas. They make ice cream in a town just up the road where they claim the cows think they're in heaven. I know why they say that. It is truly one of the loveliest parts of our state, even in the rain.

Once in Hempstead, I found Wolfram's and stopped in there to see Mr. Wolfram. A salesperson told me he was at lunch and gave me directions to the restaurant. It wasn't hard to find. Hempstead wasn't exactly a huge place.

I found him at a nice little diner called Goodman's. He was seated at a table with two other women and a small child. He was a nice man of about fifty-five, portly with a bald head and a funny gray handlebar mustache.

"Mr. Wolfram?"

"Yes."

"I'm Toni Sullivan. Nadine Ferguson gave me your name and said you might me able to help me. I'm the forensic sculptor who reconstructed Brian's image."

"Oh my! How nice to meet you."

He stood up and we shook hands.

"Call me Bud, Toni."

"Nice to meet you, Bud."

"You'll be interested in meeting my friends here. These are two good friends of Brian's. Julie Paine and Frances Holman, she used to be Frances Miller."

I couldn't believe my luck. Julie Paine still looked like the young girl she must have been when Brian Ferguson was alive. She was a plain woman with fair skin, a small upturned nose, large, blue eyes with a sad appearance in them and a sweet, but tentative, smile. Her fine blond hair was tied in a ponytail with a green ribbon that matched the shirt she wore. Frances Holman Miller was a large-boned woman with tanned skin and she appeared to be fit. She had short black hair, a long slender nose and deep brown eyes, with an air of confidence Julie seemed to lack.

I shook both their hands, and Bud asked me to join them. It suited me just fine, I was starving for lunch myself. I sat down and ordered something to eat.

"The police asked us if we recognized that other woman who was killed," Julie said.

"We didn't," Frances continued.

"We knew everyone Brian knew," Mr. Wolfram offered. "He was just a really high-quality person. He really only wanted a simple life here. With his credentials he could have been teaching some-where, but he wanted to live simply and study birds."

"Yes, his mother told me. She told me he traveled from time to time to other places to study."

"Yes. That was how he spent his vacation time. I was very lenient with his time off because he was just such a great guy—such a great friend."

He looked down at the table. I noticed that Julie looked very sad and upset. Before I could think of anything wonderful to say, a man in police uni-form came up to the table. He greeted everyone there.

"Who's your friend here?" he said, referring to me.

"I'm so sorry," Bud said. "Toni Sullivan, this is Chief Grant. He's the head of our police department."

"It's nice to meet you, Chief."

"Toni Sullivan? You're the artist, the one who did Brian's sculpture."

"Yes," I said, surprised that he could remember my name.

"I met your son, so to speak. He and his partner and I spent some time talking about the case over the phone."

"Oh, I see."

"So, what brings you down here?"

"Chief, pull up a chair and join us," Bud said.

He pulled up a chair, and began asking me questions.

"Your son and his partner asked me questions about Brian and some woman name Addie Waldrep. They faxed me her photo, but she didn't look familiar to me, and I don't know any folks around here named Waldrep. They didn't tell me a whole lot about what was going on, though. Who was this Addie Waldrep, and what does she have to do with Brian?"

Julie looked more upset now. I wasn't sure if Tommy and Mike would approve of me telling them this, but I wasn't going to sit there and watch this young woman unravel on me.

"Actually, at this point, we don't know that she had anything to do with Brian. Her bones were found in a similar manner in Austin, so the police are trying to get any information they can on how and why the killer did these things."

"I see. Then who was she?"

"She was actually a woman who went missing from a small town not far from Austin. She's been missing for sixteen years. Another man from her town went missing about the same time."

"Huh. So, there must have been some similarity in the way they were killed or something that made y'all think they were linked."

"Yes. Their remains were in a similar condition and left in similar circumstances. We don't think Austin is their original burial place."

"So, the woman's remains were found in a similar manner to Brian's?" he mused out loud.

"Yes, her bones were found dumped in a fresh grave along the riverbank on what we call Red Bud Isle. If they hadn't been found by a passing kayaker that morning, they probably would have gone undiscovered until they were carried away by the spring rains."

"Interesting," he said, leaning back precariously in the diner chair. "Then where were Brian's remains found in relation to hers?"

"His were actually quite a ways downstream near a running trail that crosses a creek that feeds into the river. His remains really weren't close to the water at all. They were actually surprisingly close to this running trail."

"Uh-huh. So, y'all think because they were both reburied like that and the bones all jumbled up like, that's why the two deaths are related?"

"Well, and also because the soil samples on both point to an original burial in this area."

"Hmm. I'll be." He landed the chair back on the floor and shook his head in amazement.

"That's really what brings me down here."

"How's that?"

"Well, I've been visiting with Nadine Ferguson to try to find out where some of Brian's favorite bird-watching spots were, but she couldn't remember. She thought that Bud, Julie and Frances could help me with that."

"Why do you think that would help?" Julie asked.

"Well, if he went bird-watching right before he disappeared—and I had heard that is what he was doing—then maybe we could narrow down some spots where he might have been killed. There might be something in that location that would give us more clues to go on. Actually, anything might help at this point."

"You know, he went to a lot of places around here, and I'm afraid my memory of exact locations wouldn't be real good," Bud said.

Julie and Frances looked at each other. The chief caught the look, as did I.

"If you two ladies have anything to say, I'd say it now. You never know what might help this lady. If you help her, you're helping Brian," Chief Grant said.

"Brian had two or three favorite places, but I think he went to the Gunther place that weekend," Julie said. "Out at Angler's Point."

She and Frances exchanged glances.

"We know that's where he went," Frances said. "The bird he was looking for was there in abundance, and he liked the place anyway."

"The Gunther place? That's over three hundred acres," the chief said. "Toni, we could never search that whole place."

"I know the places Brian went when he went there," Julie said.

"Still, we can't just walk on," Chief Grant said. "The man who owns that place now is a crotchety old guy. He would never let us on there just to look. He's got No Trespassing signs everywhere, and rumor has it that he shoots at anybody he catches on his property."

"It's true," Bud said. "He does shoot at people. He shot at the Stone boy once when he snuck on. His parents almost killed him when they found out."

"We'd have to get a warrant," the chief said. "Do you think you have enough probable cause for a warrant, Toni?"

"I don't know," I said. "But probably not."

I ran my hand through my hair. I knew we didn't have enough for a warrant. I was already thinking about talking to Drew about all of this.

"Well, that's just the pits," Bud said. "How much do you need to convince a judge?"

"Probably a lot more than they've got," Chief Grant said.

"Well, let me get back to Austin, and talk to the detectives working this case," I said. "Maybe there's something we can do."

Julie and Frances exchanged looks again, but this time I wasn't sure I understood those looks. Those two were close, I could tell, and they had their own language.

"Do you have a card, Toni?" the chief asked.

"Sure."

"If anything comes up on my end, I could give you a shout. I've already got your son's number, but if I can't reach him, I could probably reach him through you, I bet." He smiled.

"That's for sure. If nothing else, he comes over to raid the cookie jar on a regular basis."

The group chuckled. I gave the chief my card and said my goodbyes to them all. As I drove back to Austin that afternoon, I wondered about Julie and Frances and that last look.

I was grumpy when I got back to Austin. I was frustrated about knowing where we could search and not being able to go search it now. I thought there would probably be something at the original burial site that would help us, if we could just find it.

I tried to reach Drew and Mike and Tommy. None of them were in, or answering their cell phones. That just made me grumpier.

The CILHI sculpture stared at me with partial clay on it and beckoned for me to get on with it, but I was stalling. And I didn't know why I was stalling. Normally, working on something like this would take my mind off the frustration of the Red Bud and Waller Creek cases. I might even have a breakthrough on them, while working on another bust, but I couldn't get into anything. I was about to give up on the whole rest of the day and just go drink hot tea in the living room and stare out the window, when the phone rang.

Drew Smith was returning my call.

"So, you're back from Houston," he said.

"Houston and Hempstead. I made a side trip based on info I got from Nadine Ferguson."

"Did you find out anything?"

"Found two women who were good friends of Brian's. They claim to know where he went to bird-watch that last day."

"That could be helpful."

"It would be except the old coot who owns the place now apparently lets no one on his property for any reason, and shoots at people who violate his No Trespassing signs."

"Maybe I could talk him into it," Drew said. "Otherwise, we'd need a search warrant, which I don't think we could get right now."

"Right."

"The woman's information isn't concrete. He could have said he was going there, and gone somewhere else. Do Mike and Tommy have any other evidence leading to that area, or indicating a specific location?"

"None."

"I could try to finesse it out of the old man," Drew said, "and if I strike out, I could see if I can get a warrant out of a judge I know down there, but I'd have to really work it. I'm going to talk to Mike and Tommy about this now. I think there's enough reason for me to become involved. It's more than one murder, probably both committed outside of Austin, with linking crimes in Austin."

"I can't get hold of either one of them, so you'll have to brief them on my trip."

"I can handle that. Meanwhile, I have something for you."

"Oh?"

"Lisa Wells's mother was so grateful for your work on our cottonwood case that she wrote you a letter and posted it to me for delivery to you. Want me to fax it over? I can give you the original next time I see you."

"Yes, definitely fax it on."

"Okay, it'll be coming across in just a minute. I'll

try to get in touch with Tommy and Mike. We'll let you know what we decide to do."

"Thanks, Drew."

Within a minute or so, my fax machine came to life and hummed and beeped as the page came through. I pulled it off the machine and read:

Dear Dr. Sullivan,
Words could never express what you have done for me and for my family with your artwork. The bust you did of my Lisa was so beautiful and done with such care, it was as if you knew her in life. The re-semblance was perfect. You had even caught that little gleam of joy that used to be hers before she got caught up with the wrong man. Truly, you and she must have made a spiritual connection for you to see in her bones so much of what was really Lisa. Lieutenant Smith says that you are a Christian woman and that you pray often. I can only say that I was not surprised, for to see your work and have the benefit of it in this way was to share in the grace of God's gifts and comfort. May He always bless you.
Sincerely,
Gladys Wells

I forgot about frustration and self-pity. I sat and felt ashamed of myself for about five minutes, and then I got my rear in gear and got to work on the

CILHI bust. It was near to being finished and I had a responsibility to other people. It was time to do as Reverend Iordani had repeatedly advised me. It was time to focus on someone other than myself. It was time to think about Irini and her family.

I worked all night, and as I laid the clay between every tissue-depth marker, the reality of the face of this man began to be obvious. Before I went further, constructing the nose or doing anything that required intuition or judgment of my own, I wanted Chris Nakis to look at the photographs of the skull and the work I had done so far. I wanted a trained forensic anthropologist, who had never seen Ted Nikolaides, to give me her expert opinion. About seven o'clock in the morning, I stopped where I was and made the call. Chris would leave work early and come by. I told her I would make dinner for both of us.

When Chris arrived I showed her into the studio, gave her all of my photographs and notes and left her there to work while I cooked our dinner.

I had decided to make a spicy eggplant dish that I loved, and serve it with a Greek spinach and rice dish that I knew Chris loved. We would have rosemary bread and peppered olive oil.

When dinner was finally ready and on the table, I called for Chris. In a few minutes, she came out of my studio and handed me a rough drawing.

"That's what I'd do, if it were mine," she said.

She had reviewed the photos and all my notes and had checked the tissue depths I had calculated and looked at the bust where it was now. The drawing she made was of the face totally reconstructed with nose and eyes. Her work was rough, but good enough for me to get the idea. I looked at her sketch and sat down at the table. My hand was shaking.

"What is it?" Chris asked.

"This is Teddy," I said.

My eyes welled up with tears and I bit my lip and shook it off. I handed the sketch back to her and got up and walked to look out the back window. I stood there with my hands on my hips and tried to remember how to breathe.

"Well," Chris said softly, "I guess I haven't lost my skills."

We were both silent for a while. Finally, I turned around from the windows and came to the table to sit down.

"Let's eat," I said.

We said our thanksgiving over the food and dug in.

"What's next?" Chris asked.

"I'll finish it tomorrow," I said. "Thanks for your help."

"Anytime, my friend, anytime."

Chapter Fourteen

In one of the older neighborhoods in Austin, not far from my favorite cypress grove on the river trail, is an old house turned restaurant. It's called Maddie's Breakfast. Maddie's is open 24/7. She serves up eggs just about any way you can imagine them, bacon and sausage for all the carnivores, toast, waffles, pancakes, French toast, fruit dishes—and the list goes on.

Austin's own brand of music plays over the sound system—music that includes country-western, progressive country, blues and some "Austin" music that simply defies categorization. The decor is eclectic for kicked-backed comfort.

Jack and I used to take Mike there from the time he was about twelve. Now, over fifteen years later,

Mike and I still met there for an early-morning breakfast sometimes. This time we included Tommy Lucero.

I had slipped into my jeans, a cotton purple short-sleeve sweater and my brown snakeskin boots. I had made a copy of Chris's sketch with my computer printer, folded it and stuck it in my jeans pocket. I locked everything up and jumped into the Jeep to head for my breakfast appointment with my two favorite cops.

I had finished the carburetor overhaul on the Jeep and a couple of other things I was doing to it, so I had decided to take it out for my breakfast jaunt instead of the Mustang. It ran like a top. Sometimes, my mechanical abilities amazed even me. It was raining again that morning, so it was a good morning to give the Mustang a rest. The rain pounded down on the soft top of the Jeep, but my mud tires held the road well.

The boys were already there when I arrived and Tommy was "champing at the bit," as we say down here in Texas. He would have to "champ" awhile longer, because there was a twenty-minute wait and Mike and Tommy only had us on the list for five minutes when I got there. Drew had talked to both of them, but we chatted about nonsense while we waited—we didn't want anyone to overhear any of our conversation about the investigation. In ten minutes' time, they had managed to come up with a booth and they seated us.

I had already decided I was having the whole-grain French toast with fresh berries and all-natural maple syrup. I was also having an extralarge glass of their mango-tangerine juice and their awesome bottomless cup of coffee. The boys were loading up on cheesy omelettes with lots of pig meat on the side. We were all going to need an extra hour in the gym that day.

I pulled the copy of the sketch out of my jeans pocket and handed it across the table to Mike.

"That's the sketch Chris did last night of the CILHI project I'm working on. She used my notes and photos and the partially completed bust. She added the nose and eyes and finishing touches herself."

I saw the expression on Mike's face, and so did Tommy.

"What?" Tommy asked.

"I've seen pictures of Uncle Teddy my whole life. He was shot down before Mom and Dad even married. But I'd know this face anywhere. Chris has never seen Uncle Teddy, has she?"

I shook my head.

Mike looked at Tommy. "This is my Uncle Ted." Mike looked back at me. "You finished with the bust yet?"

"I'll finish it after breakfast. I could see where it was going, but I wanted Chris to work blind and show me what she thought it should look like."

"Wow," Mike said under his breath. "Mom, they really found him this time, didn't they?"

"Yes, son, they really, finally found him."

Tommy was looking at the sketch and shaking his head.

"Toni, how long has he been missing?"

"Since June 30, 1968."

"That's over thirty years ago."

"Yes."

Mike handed me the sketch and I put it back in my jeans pocket. Our food arrived and we all dug in.

"So, Toni, give us your take on the trip to Houston and Hempstead," Tommy said. "Drew talked to us yesterday, but I want to hear all the details."

I was about halfway through my French toast, but I began to tell Mike and Tommy about my conversation with Nadine. First I told them about seeing Lori Webster on Mrs. Ferguson's street. I told them I wasn't a hundred percent sure, but I was pretty sure it was her.

"Mike and I will go back up to Georgetown and talk to her again."

Then I told them about Nadine and the Hempstead group.

"Nadine didn't know any spots where her son bird-watched, or if she did, she couldn't remember. She gave me the names of three of his friends in Hempstead. Two you had already talked to."

"Julie and Frances?" Tommy asked.

"Right."

"And?" Mike said expectantly.

"And a guy named Bud Wolfram. He was Brian's boss. Before I got down to all my questions, the local police chief came in and joined us."

"Chief Grant," Tommy said.

"Right. He asked me some questions."

"Okay," Tommy said. "So what did Julie and Frances tell you exactly?"

"Well, Julie started by telling me that she knew several places, but couldn't be sure about the exact one. Then she and Frances exchanged a look, and Frances told me they knew exactly where he had been that day."

"So, it was this place Drew told us about," Mike said. "Some cranky old guy owns it and won't let us on."

"Well, that's what Chief Grant says. Bud Wolfram said the old guy shot at some kid who trespassed. Apparently the whole place is marked No Trespassing and he shoots on sight, no questions asked."

"Drew said he called Chief Grant yesterday after the two of you talked," Mike said.

"Oh?"

"Yeah, the chief went out there yesterday and the old guy told him no one was coming on to his property for any reason. It would be a cold day in July before he let the police search there for anything. Then he started raving about knowing his rights."

"Great."

"So, we are definitely going to need a warrant, and it'll need to be airtight or we're hosed," Tommy said.

"What else did you talk about with Mrs. Ferguson? Was that it?" Mike asked.

"No, son. We had a mothers' and widows' conversation that I thought was more appropriate. She showed me Brian's sketches and a book he wrote. He had a doctorate in ornithology."

"Whoa! I didn't know that," Tommy said.

"Yes, so that's what all the bird watching was about. All his friends talk about what a nice guy he was."

Tommy continued. "Yeah, we got the same impression of him. Mrs. Ferguson had talked to him on the phone the day before he disappeared. He was good about calling her regularly. They were apparently a pretty close family and kept in touch. He would go to Houston about once a month, even though he really didn't like it there."

"Does anyone like Houston?" Mike asked.

"Mike..."

"Well, Mom..."

"Tommy, go on."

Tommy was smiling as he swallowed a bite of his omelette. "She said he had called her the night before. Said he was going out the next day—his day off—to do some bird watching in the surrounding countryside. He was really excited about it because he'd been working a lot and was looking forward to being outside and relaxing."

"So, he went alone? I wonder why the girls didn't go?"

"Actually, Mrs. Ferguson said he was looking forward to going alone and having some time to himself."

"Did anyone check with the two girls when he didn't come back—I mean, at the time?"

"Yeah. There was a search for him and he was never found. The two girls had totally solid alibis and were not suspects. In fact, from the way she tells it, they were devastated by his disappearance."

"Yes, Nadine Ferguson told me that part. She said Julie was interested in him."

"Apparently he was interested in her, too, Mom. She never really got over him."

We finished our breakfasts and then the boys and I fought over the check, but Tommy won. It would be the Sullivans' turn next time.

It was still raining steadily, but not heavily. I was frustrated by these two cases in Austin and troubled by the CILHI case, and the weather was not improving my mood. I drove off through the damp and gloom thinking about Addie Waldrep, Brian Ferguson and Doug Hughes, and wondering if we would ever know the truth.

On my way home I had turned off the beaten path and headed toward the cemetery without even giving it much thought. I arrived at the stoplight outside the front gates, wondering if I were going to go on in or not. The light turned green and I proceeded through the gates. I drove slowly along the narrow road inside, winding my way through various sections until I came to the section where Jack was buried. There was a grove of trees nearby, and their foliage spread shade over the grave site—at least they did on a sunny day. I parked the car along the roadside and got out.

It was misting now, and I was wearing a rain slicker I had grabbed from the back seat of the car. I walked carefully through the graves and approached Jack's plot. I looked down at the tombstone—"John 'Jack' Kevin Sullivan." Every time I looked at it, I had the same incredulous feeling—the feeling that it couldn't be, that someone had gotten it wrong somehow. Emotion gave way to intellect, though, and I knew it was true.

I sat on a stone bench that Mike and I had placed next to the grave.

"I came to tell you that they finally found Ted's remains in 'Nam. Guess you already knew, but I just found out."

The mist tapered off a bit, and there was a slight rustling in the tree above me. I saw a sparrow huddled up under some leaves. I looked back down at Jack's headstone.

"Irini asked me to help identify Ted. I didn't want to, but I didn't have a choice. They were having trouble with it because of his DNA, and because his teeth were so good. It was hard, Jack. I got Chris to help me some, and now I have to go home and finish up the work."

A car drove by slowly and then came to a stop up ahead at the next section of graves. I looked down at my hands and cleared my throat.

"Anyway, I guess you know I was real upset with you the other day for leaving me to deal with it all by myself, but ever since then, it's been a little better. So, I guess you were praying for me over there, the way I do for you over here. I'm sorry. Sometimes I get to missing you so much that I forget what we both believe. I'm doing the best I can, Jack. I hope you'll cut me some slack when I lose it over you."

Another car pulled up behind mine and two women got out and started walking in my direction—obviously coming to visit a grave somewhere near Jack's.

"Well, I have to go now. I have to finish Ted's reconstruct. Go with me, Jack, and keep praying for me. I can't have you with me physically right now, but I need to know you're there spiritually."

I said, "May your memory be eternal."

I went back to the Jeep, cranked it over and drove carefully out and headed home.

When I got back to the house, I went into my studio straightaway to do what I knew I had to do. I sat looking at the partially finished face. It looked like a skeleton with muscle laid over it. It didn't look like anyone in particular at this point, but Chris had made her sketch of the finished face with eyes and nose. Now I had to get my hands back into the clay, adding the final layer of "flesh," including eyes instead of clay sockets, and a nose that extended beyond the bone below the flesh. Finally, I began to smooth the final layer of clay, adding those last sculptural touches that made it human. I added clay hair to the bust, parting it and creating texture in it to mimic Ted's hair in its short military cut. Now it was done.

I sat on the stool for a while and just stared. I stared at a face I had not seen like this in over thirty years. But I had known as soon as I had put my hands on that skull in Hawaii that it was Ted. I could feel it—and I could even see it in the bone structure itself. I had to know if what I had seen in that skull was real or just what I wanted to see. That's why I had Chris come and verify everything I had done and finish the bust for me, before I actually finished it in clay. Even then, with Chris's blind input and the finished bust before me, I hardly believed that those meager remains belonged to my friend Ted. At that moment, looking at that face, I felt strangely numb. The feelings just didn't come. I guess it had just taken so long to get there, it was difficult to absorb.

Chris was going to sign an affidavit and attach her sketch to it to send with my materials to CILHI. She was a well-known and respected forensic anthropologist and medical examiner. Her certification gave my work the objectivity it needed, not just for the scientists and officials at CILHI, but for me.

I looked at the clock. It was 4:30 p.m. It was 11:30 a.m. in Hawaii. I might catch Sergeant Major Tomlinson before he went to lunch. I picked up the phone and dialed the number. They transferred me to the sergeant major's line, and he answered.

"Sergeant Major, I have finished the bust."

I first explained about the input from Dr. Nakis, and then I told the sergeant major that Dr. Nakis's affidavit would be part of the documentation I would sent to CILHI.

"And what is the result, Dr. Sullivan?"

"It is the image of Captain Theodore P. Nikolaides."

"Well, thank goodness."

It was as emotional as I ever heard the sergeant major get. Each time I had worked with him previously, we had identified the man CILHI was searching for, and each time the sergeant major had a similar response. He was a soldier through and through, but his heart was in this work for sure.

"It all sounds excellent, Dr. Sullivan. I'm sure we'll find the results satisfactory. I'm glad that we could identify Captain Nikolaides and close his case."

"Yes, so am I."

I felt odd talking about Ted as if he were a case, but the sergeant major tried to stay detached in his work. He saw hundreds of "cases." He had one disappointment after another in those cases when ID's could not be made. He allowed himself one heartfelt expression of relief, and then he was back to business. I wondered what, if any, emotion he allowed himself in private.

"If you would, Dr. Sullivan, send all your materials—notes, photos, Dr. Nakis's affidavit—send all that to me. Dr. Carroway and his team will review everything and make an official determination as soon as they can."

"Any idea how long it will take, Sergeant Major?"

"I would say at least two weeks, Doctor."

"Very well, then I would like to request permission to tell Mrs. Nikolaides the results—unofficially, of course. It would really be impossible for me to keep the information from her."

"Of course, that's fine, as long as she and you understand that the results are not official until they are declared so by CILHI."

"Yes. We both understand that."

"Another nice job, Dr. Sullivan. Thank you for your time and dedication to these projects."

"It is always my privilege, Sergeant Major."

We said our goodbyes and hung up. My next call was to Reverend Iordani. I wanted to go and tell Irini, but I didn't want to do it by myself. Besides, I thought she should have a minister there for her when she got this news. Reverend Iordani answered the phone on the second ring.

"Reverend, it's Toni."

"Oh, Toni, how is everything going?"

"I finished the bust on the CILHI case, and it is Ted Nikolaides."

"Ohhh…" He made a soft clicking noise with his tongue. "Well, I guess even though it's sad, it's a good thing now that we know. Bittersweet, though. Are you okay?"

"Yes, Reverend, I'm fine."

I actually wasn't sure how I was, but I didn't want to get into a protracted discussion of all that now.

"Reverend, I need to go and tell Irini and I want to tell her in person. Can you go with me, say, later this afternoon?"

"If you can wait until about four, I can go."

"I think that will be fine, Reverend."

"Then meet me at four at the Chuck Wagon out on Highway 71. Do you know where that is?"

"Yes, I know exactly where it is. I'll see you there."

I said goodbye and we hung up.

I was glad to have it all done. Glad it was over now. Glad that I had Chris's work to back me up.

There was still this frustration over Addie Waldrep's and Brian Ferguson's deaths, though. It was eating at me more than ever. Now that Ted's status was confirmed, all I had unresolved was finding the murderer of Addie and Brian, and determining the whereabouts of Doug Hughes.

I closed the studio door once again. I needed to pray. There was so much death around me lately, and the evil that had caused those untimely deaths had unbalanced what little inner stillness I had. I would pray for a while—for Ted's soul, and to try to reclaim my peace and harmony with the Creator—to put the evil out of my mind and keep it from infecting my peace. By then, it would be time to clean up, so I could rendezvous with Reverend Iordani.

I met Reverend Iordani at the Chuck Wagon right on time. It was on the highway between Austin and Dripping Springs. Dripping Springs was a little bedroom community outside of Austin, and it was where Irini Nikolaides made her home. Irini lived on a three-acre spread where she grew vegetables in her own garden and made baked goods for a local bakery. She also raised goats and had a thriving goat dairy.

I parked in the lot at the Chuck Wagon and went inside. It was a dive, but they had great coffee and that was why Reverend Iordani loved this place. We sat down and had a cup together, and I told him about the bust of Ted.

"So, then, we're sure it's him?"

"Yes," I said. Then I told him about Chris's part in the reconstruction.

He nodded. "Well, that's it, then. She didn't even know him."

"No, she didn't."

"Let's go. I'll call Irini and tell her I'll be there in five minutes."

We got into Reverend Iordani's car and he called Irini. After he hung up, we said a prayer and headed for Irini's place.

When we pulled up to the gate, Irini was there to open it. Irini was so short, she barely cleared the top of the gate. She may have been small, but she was strong enough to swing that heavy gate open all by herself. Dad said she had the map of Greece on her face because of her large nose and full lips, but she was Greek from head to toe with her stocky build. It had not been that long since I had seen her, but she seemed much older now. Her dark hair had been peppered with gray for years, but now there were more lines in her olive skin and the light in her dark eyes seemed to have dimmed. She saw me in the front seat and her expression darkened immediately. We pulled up to the house, and as we got out of Reverend Iordani's car, Irini walked up to greet us. She kissed Reverend Iordani's hand in greeting and asked for a blessing, which he gave readily. We all hugged and then went inside.

"I know I should wait until I serve you some coffee and something to eat, but I can't," she said. "You must tell me now. I know that's why you are here. It is either bad news or worse news, so tell me."

Reverend Iordani looked at me. He was there with me, but he clearly indicated to me with his look that he thought it was my responsibility to tell her what my findings were. He was right. I had made the ID, with Chris's support, and it was my job to tell her.

"Irini, I have finished the work. Before I finished it, I had Chris Nakis come and check what I had done and give me her opinion. Her opinion matched what I thought. Irini, CILHI has found Teddy."

She stood before us for what seemed like minutes, but I know it was only two or three seconds. Then she clutched Reverend Iordani's shoulder and cried out with the pain she had held for all those years. It was the sound that reflected what we all had known was true, but it was also the sound of hope at last abandoned. She sobbed and Reverend Iordani held her and comforted her. I moved in behind her and put my arm around her shoulder. The three of us stood there in a huddle and there was no sound between us all, except for Irini's crying and her mumbled Greek that I didn't understand. I don't know how I did it, but somehow strength and composure was mine—or at least God let me believe that it was mine.

∽ Chapter Fifteen ∽

It was another day of rain and gloom. The rain was actually pleasant, soft and steady and much needed if the bluebonnets were going to flourish this year. Without the thunder, lightning and high winds of a typical Texas storm, this was actually soothing, and I needed soothing. I stood at the back French doors with hot chamomile tea and watched the rain nourish every green and budding thing in the backyard.

The question of Ted's death was solved. It still saddened me, and all that sadness was compounded by the unresolved murders of Addie Waldrep and Brian Ferguson. I reflected on my conversations with Drew and hoped that his connections and his efforts could yield a warrant to search the Gunther place.

It was time to focus on something other than death. I put on some jeans and an old navy blue T-shirt with my black pointy-toe boots. I got into the Mustang, fired it up and headed over to Daddy's.

Daddy was eighty-three. He was a mechanic and welder, and just a guy who could fix or build anything. His name was Michael Kennedy—yes, I named my son after him—but the world called him Red because of the color his hair used to be. Like mine, the gray had come into his hair and rendered it more the shade of pink champagne. Mine wasn't quite that extreme yet, but I was on my way there. Mom was gone to the other side and had been for years. Daddy lived alone, but kept himself busy with friends, automotive work and the Mustang club and classic car restorations.

When I pulled up into the driveway, the garage door was open and Daddy was where I expected him to be—under a car. He heard the rumble of my Fastback and rolled out from under the car to see me step out. He got up off the creeper and headed for the Go-Jo canister to clean his hands. The Go-Jo having successfully removed all the grease, Daddy came to greet me, wiping his hands on a red shop rag.

"Little Red!"

"Hi, Daddy."

He gave me a big hug and said, "Where's my grandson?"

"He's working, Daddy."

"Boy's always on duty. He comes by a lot, but he's always on duty. Can't get that boy out of a suit long enough to change a spark plug."

"It's his job, Daddy, and it's not an eight-to-five gig."

"I know, I would just like to spend some time with him, that's all. Never mind all that, my Little Red is here. What's happening with you, kiddo?"

"Well, Daddy, Irini called me a few weeks ago, and asked me to do a reconstruct on some remains CILHI found in 'Nam."

"Know that already. Mike told me."

"Oh, didn't know you had talked to Mike lately."

"Like I said, he comes by. He don't ever stay, and he don't ever help me out here, but he comes by. Chews the fat with his old grandpa—you know." Daddy beamed as he got back down on the creeper and rolled under the car again.

"Hand me that light, Little Red."

I handed Daddy the light.

"So, then, what's up with all that CILHI stuff?"

"I had Chris come over and check my work when I was almost through. Still needed a nose, eyes and hair on it, but she checked everything over and drew me a rough sketch."

"Hand me that grease gun, Toni."

I handed him the grease gun.

"So, how'd Chris's drawing turn out?"

"It was him, Daddy."

"I'll be. Did you finish it all up, then?"

"Yes, sir, I finished it yesterday, and called CILHI to tell them."

"That's good, Toni. You tell Irini yet?"

"Yes, sir, I went with Reverend Iordani and told her yesterday."

Dad rolled out from under the car far enough to look me in the eye. "She take it all okay?"

"As well as anyone could take that kind of news, I suppose."

He rolled completely out from under the car with the grease gun in his hand. He got up off the creeper and hung the gun back on the hook on the wall. He turned around and put his hand on my shoulder.

"You tell her my prayers are with her."

"I will, Dad," I said with my eyes turning misty.

"Now, listen here. I know what you did was real hard, but it was necessary. You got Chris's help, which was smart. I know you did a good job, and you relieved that poor family's mind. Sometimes doing the right thing is real difficult. *Pfui,* what am I talkin' about, most of the time doing the right thing is difficult. That's why so many people these days take the lazy way out."

"I know, Daddy."

"Craziest war I ever heard of. Now, World War II—that was a war worth fightin'. Hitler, Mussolini, Japanese military—all a bunch 'a nuts trying to take over the world. We had to stop 'em. By golly, we did stop 'em, too. But, Vietnam, what a terrible waste. Send all our best young men over there, and some of our best young women, too. How many of 'em killed and still missing?"

"Over 58,000 killed, over 1,900 still missing."

"Terrible—over 58,000 killed. Craziest war I ever heard of. Wasted all those lives, ruined all those families, totally messed up our country's values—even to this day."

"I know, Dad."

"Okay, I'm talkin' too much. Just gets me upset thinking about little Irini and her family—and then I start thinking about all the other families just like hers," Dad sighed. "Tell me about your other case instead. What's going on there?"

He walked around to the front of the car and stuck his head under the hood.

"Hand me that light again, Toni."

I picked up the light off the floor and handed it to him.

"And that spark-plug wrench over there on the bench."

I handed him the spark-plug wrench.

"Well, we found bones down on Red Bud Isle..."

"I know that part. Mike told me some and I saw some of it on the news. Details, I want details."

I smiled and then I told him about Doug Hughes and Addie Waldrep. I told him about Jimmy Hughes and Lori Webster. I told him about Dody. I told him about Brian Ferguson and his mother, and what his friends in Hempstead had said. I told him everything Leo had said. I told him about Drew getting involved. I told him about Doris and the famous pie.

"Well, that all sounds real interesting—especially the part about that pie. You gotta take me up there, Little Red, introduce me to Doris and her pie," he chuckled.

I laughed, "All right, Daddy. When this case is over, I'll take you up to Viola."

"So, has Drew gotten the warrant yet?"

"Haven't heard from him, but I imagine it's going to be real hard to get, if not impossible."

"Some justice system," he said, pulling his head out from under the car hood. "Some nut with a shotgun holds up the whole works, while another nut gets by with murder."

"Well, Dad, the system is designed the way it is to protect the innocent."

"I understand all that. Still bugs me when it protects some nutball who wants to go off killin' people, and some poor kid who never did anything gets killed, breaks his mama's and daddy's hearts."

"I know, Dad."

"You say the mom is dying."

"Yes, sir."

Dad shook his head. "Sad, sad. You better catch that weirdo, Toni. Catch him and put him away."

"We're trying, Daddy. We're working as hard as we can."

"Well, I know that's right," he said, scrutinizing me with a squint. "You've got the same disease my grandson has—you work too much."

"And what are you doing out here, if not working on the neighbor's Chevrolet?"

"Aw, Toni, this is playin', not workin'. I've been playin' at this my whole life." He laughed. He laughed because he knew it wasn't true about it not being work.

"Right, Daddy."

"'Stang sounds like it's running good. You must have been keeping up with it pretty well," he said, eyeballing my Black Beauty in the driveway.

"Yeah, I tuned it up about a month or so ago, so it's in prime condition. Just did a carb overhaul on the Jeep last week."

"Well!" he said, beaming. "I'm impressed. Did that without the old man, did you?"

I laughed, "Yeah, Daddy, I did. I needed the therapy."

"Yep, know what you mean. Well, so how does it run now?"

"Great."

"Heh, you're a chip off the old block. Nice work, kiddo. I'd like to hear it run, drive it a little bit."

"Anytime you want, Dad."

"Got a son, got a grandson—neither one of 'em is worth much in the garage. Got a redheaded daughter who could overhaul any engine as well as any guy can, and better than most. Heck, I think this calls for Mexican food and a game of pool. What do you think, Little Red?"

"I'm all over that, Daddy."

My dad was like a doctor with a prescription for my mood. He was one smart old guy. He went inside and took a quick shower, while I closed up the garage for him. By the time I got inside and had washed my hands, he was in clean trousers, a plaid shirt and a lightweight jacket. He had put on socks and his work shoes again. I don't think the man owned but one pair of shoes. He liked them and that was all that mattered.

We went to Dad's favorite hole-in-the-wall Tex-Mex joint. There we ate cheesy, greasy food that I almost never eat, and talked more about my latest two cases.

"What are y'all going to do if Drew can't get that warrant to search that ol' boy's property?"

"I don't know, but we'll get the evidence eventually, and then we'll identify the killer. The last thing any of us want to do is go to trial and have the killer acquitted, so we want to be careful how we do things."

"No kidding. They did that in one of them cases up in Dallas where some ol' boy killed his wife. They went to trial, and I wondered at the time why they were in such an all-fired hurry."

I nodded. "Yeah, I remember that one, too."

"Nut can just go out into the middle of the street in downtown Dallas and confess it if he wants to. Ain't nothin' anyone can do. The law can't touch him." Daddy shook his head in disgust.

"I know, Dad, it's called double jeopardy, and that's exactly what we're trying to avoid here by being careful."

"Well, from what you tell me, that boy Brian disappeared in Hempstead, and that's where y'all think he was probably killed, along with that woman, right?"

"Yes."

"He wouldn't have had any reason to go up to Viola as far you can tell, right?"

"Right—so far anyway."

"So, what was Addie Waldrep doing in Hempstead?"

"We don't know, Dad."

"Well, I ain't no detective, but it seems to me that if a person kills someone somewhere, or buries someone somewhere, it's for a reason. I mean, he don't just throw darts at a map, right?"

"Yeah."

"So, she was there for a reason, and that's where the killer killed her with that Brian kid. What's Addie's tie to Hempstead?"

"I don't know. We've asked people in Hempstead about Addie, but no one knows her. Mike and Tommy asked, and so did I."

"Well, I don't know, Little Red, but it's got to be there somewhere. I know you'll find it."

Dad and I headed to the pool hall. We played pool until eleven o'clock that night. Daddy was just the tonic I needed to get out of the doldrums and back on track. I want to be just like him when I grow up.

The phone woke me the next morning. It sounded like a fire bell and I groaned as I rolled over to pick it up. It was Chief Grant.

"Dr. Sullivan, it's Chief Grant from Hempstead. I wanted to let you know that we've discovered some bones in a fresh shallow grave, similar to what has been found up there in Austin."

I sat up in bed.

"Old bones?"

"They appear to be."

"How were they found?"

The chief cleared his throat. "Julie and Frances went exploring on the old Gunther place at Angler's Point. They checked out all of Brian's favorite spots and found nothing, then they made a little side trip trying to get off the property and literally stumbled over this grave."

"I'd like to come down, Chief, and see the site. Who's handling the investigation?"

"I've called Lieutenant Smith with the Texas Rangers. He's on his way down."

"Good. Do you mind if I come down with him?"

"No, if he doesn't mind, then I don't. You're welcome to come on down and see this."

After I hung up with the chief, I virtually leaped out of bed. I started to run for the shower and then I decided I'd call Drew first, then Mike, but before I could call anyone, the phone rang again.

"Toni. Drew."

"Tell me that you're calling because you want me to come with you to Hempstead."

"I am. Chief Grant already call you?"

"He did."

"I want you to do the reconstruct on this one. If you want to ride with me, you'll have to be ready in twenty minutes."

"Come on by. Oh, could you call my son and let him know?"

"I've already done that, Toni."

I loved the efficiency of Drew Smith. I hung up and ran for the shower. Another great thing about having short hair is the five-minute shower. I dried off, slapped on the bare minimum of makeup just so I wouldn't scare small children or animals, combed my hair and put on my jeans, a brown cotton sweater and my brown snakeskin boots, grabbed a jacket and dashed outside to wait on the curb for Drew.

We talked about the case on the way down. Drew had beaten his head against a wall to try to get a warrant, but he had not been able to do so. The old coot who owned the property, Mr. Burkhardt, was apparently as mad as a wet hen, and wanted to press trespassing charges against Julie and Frances. The chief, with Drew's instruction, had informed Mr. Burkhardt that trespassing or not, two citizens had reported finding a skeleton on his property, and that he could either cooperate or a warrant would be obtained and his property forcibly searched. The old man had relented. No trespassing charges would be pressed. Access to his property had been granted.

"I had no luck tracking the whereabouts of Doug Hughes, but I'd bet credits to navy beans those two women just found him," Drew said.

"I agree, but we'll need proof to back up that assumption."

"That's why you're here," Drew said and smiled.

"Chief Grant said this wasn't exactly where the women were looking."

"It wasn't, which explains why nothing was found when they searched for Brian sixteen years ago. Apparently, Julie and Frances looked in all Brian's old haunts and then decided to take what the chief referred to as 'one of Brian's alternate trails' out of the property."

"Good grief."

"Yeah. Julie fell over the grave mound and when she fell, the heel of her hand dug into the soft mud and exposed part of an arm bone."

"Yippee."

"Oh yeah. Shocked her totally and it was all they could do to get out of there fast enough. Chief Grant said when they got to his office, they were both muddy and pretty messed up otherwise, too."

"What they did was either incredibly brave or incredibly stupid."

"Well, I think just a little of both, but I'm so grateful to both of 'em, I really don't care."

"Amen."

Drew had talked to Mike and Tommy to let them know what was going on. They were coming down and would meet us there.

Chief Grant had given Drew precise instructions on how to get there. We arrived at the gate of a farm the chief had referred to as "the old Gunther place." Apparently, the Gunther family had owned the land for years and all the locals referred to it that way, even though someone else had bought it and now lived there. Old Mr. Gunther had been a nice man, according to what the chief had told Drew. It was a large property and trespassers in his woods were common, but Mr. Gunther didn't care, as long as they stayed out of his fields and didn't damage anything or do anything illegal there. Mr. Burkhardt had a totally opposite opinion to Mr. Gunther. Regardless of his wishes, Julie and Frances had trespassed, and had found more than they bargained for, and exactly what we had hoped to find.

When we arrived, I was relieved to see the State Crime Lab folks were already on the scene and had it under control. Drew had told the chief not to touch anything and to keep the scene guarded and secure until they could get there. He had dispatched the crime lab people immediately and they were hard at work.

We had parked the car at the end of a dirt road that led around the edge of the property and had walked the rest of the way into the woods to the spot. One of Chief Grant's men had been waiting for us and led us in. As we walked up onto the site, I witnessed the same archaeological methods I had seen applied in Austin in the removal of these bones.

We greeted Chief Grant and he gave us the rundown.

"The two women came out to this place because they heard that we weren't able to get a warrant. They were frustrated, so they took matters into their own hands. It didn't quite turn out the way they expected, but all's well, etcetera."

"I hear the trespassing charges were dropped," I said, smiling.

The chief rolled his eyes. "Crazy old guy was going to throw a monkey wrench into the whole works with all that nonsense. I made it clear to him that we were going to investigate this report with or without his permission. His wife is the one who talked sense to him." The chief smiled. "She told him how the cow ate the cabbage, and that was it."

"Good," I said.

"The women tell me this was one of Brian's alternate routes off of the property. He would occasionally come out this way after a bird-watching jaunt."

"I'll want to question those women, Chief," Drew said.

"I know. I have them down at the station with one of my men. I've told them they'd have to wait for you before they could go home. I just didn't want them out here watching all this, so I made them stay in town."

"That's fine. I'll talk to them first and then I want to come back out here and talk to the owner of this place before I leave."

"No problem," Chief Grant said.

I moved closer to the site and looked at the grave that was being unearthed. It looked as though a larger area had been dug up and the soil replaced, but only this part was mounded up for the grave. I wondered if this was the site of the original burials. It would explain the larger area where the earth had obviously been disturbed.

"Chief, this larger area where the dirt has obviously been recently disturbed, has this been looked at? Is this something that Burkhardt did?"

"I asked him about that and he says he hasn't even been to these woods in as long as seven or eight months. He rides out here occasionally, but he's getting real old and doesn't come out as often he used to."

I looked back at the dig area. The bones had been dumped—jumbled just like the other two sites. Why would the bones have been removed and reburied like this?

"Drew, I want copies of the photos your lab folks have taken here."

"No problem, but why do you want them?"

"I'm going to show them to Leo Driskill."

"Sure. That's fine. I'll make sure you get a set."

"Thanks."

The scene enthralled me. I locked on to it visually, but really emotionally. I knew this had to be the original burial site. The murderer had buried his victims here and then come back to unearth them, moving at least two of them. He probably murdered them here as well.

"Drew, this is probably the site of the murders, don't you think?"

"Yes, I do."

Blood had been spilled here—the blood of three people. What kind of person could do that? How do you kill three people and then bury their bloody bodies in a mass grave like this? I stood and pondered it all for a while. I couldn't imagine the killer's rage in doing this, or the fear Addie must have felt to know that he was going to kill them. I thought of Brian probably struggling to get away before he was killed. That's probably why he was shot so many times, and not shot in the head. I shuddered to think of all of it. The evil of that place hung like a death shroud there. Then I wondered if anyone would ever know the truth about Addie and Doug, and what had happened here, or if the mystery would be eternal.

"You need to get those soil samples to the same folks at A&M that Chris was working with."

"I'm already on that, too, Toni." He smiled.

I sighed. "Sorry. It's just that I've been looking for some break in this case and I haven't been able to come up with anything. Now, this looks like the original site…"

Drew patted me on the shoulder. "I know. Your problem is, you don't know how to deal with a case that has you stumped." He chuckled.

"Well, I get involved with people when I rebuild their faces."

"I know."

Mike and Tommy had arrived and were shown in. They looked over my way and nodded and then checked everything out for themselves. They spoke with a couple of the forensic techs and then came over to where Drew and I were standing.

"This is it, isn't it, Toni?" Tommy asked.

"Yes."

"You doing the reconstruct, Mom?"

"Yes. That's why Drew brought me down here—well, it's the main reason anyway."

"We're going to town in just a minute and question the two women who found the grave. I'm sure you two will want to go with us," Drew said.

"Absolutely," Tommy replied.

We talked amongst ourselves a few more minutes, then Drew gave final instructions to the lab people, and he, Mike, Tommy and I went back into town with Chief Grant.

The women had been held waiting a long time. They were tired, but worse yet, they were very emotionally shaken. The two were still recovering from the remains of their friend, Brian, being found. Even though it had been their conscious choice to go looking for "evidence" on the old Gunther farm, neither woman had expected to stumble over a skeleton. While viewing skeletal remains might be a common occurrence for me, it was definitely a pretty unsettling event for most people.

Drew was now working the case with Mike and Tommy, but he had asked them if they would let him lead the questioning of the women. When he was done with all his questions, they could add any that he hadn't covered. He didn't have to ask them if this was all right—Mike and Tommy had no jurisdiction in this part of the world, but Drew asked anyway. That was just Drew Smith's way.

When we walked into the chief's office, the two women were sitting with the patrolman on duty at the front desk. They had been provided with hot tea and they looked as though they were in need of that and some bourbon. We took both of them into the chief's private office.

Drew began, "Ladies, first of all you both did us a favor by finding and reporting the skeleton on Mr. Burkhardt's property, but you are very lucky that he did not shoot you, or file charges against you."

The two women glanced at one another with concern.

"We know that, Lieutenant," Julie said, "but we were not going to let that old man and his stubbornness stop the progress in finding Brian's killer."

"Right," Frances chimed in. "So, does the skeleton we found have anything to do with it all?"

"We don't know for sure yet," Drew said, "but it probably does. Dr. Sullivan here will be able to help us with that. She's going to give the deceased his or her face back. Then we can begin to answer some questions."

"I guess the finding of this skeleton could just be some kind of weird coincidence, though, huh?" Julie asked.

"I suppose it could be, Miss Paine," Drew responded, "but I personally don't believe in weird coincidences—particularly when it involves old skeletons in parts of the world where a murdered man and woman are known to have been previously buried."

Julie looked upset now and stared down at her tea mug. Frances reached over and squeezed her hand.

"I'm sorry, Miss Paine, I didn't mean to upset you," Drew said.

"Oh no, it's not your fault," she said shakily. "It's just thinking of poor Brian..."

Now she began to cry and Frances put her arm around her.

"It's not your fault, Lieutenant," Frances said. "This is why I went with her. We had to try. We had to do something. Brian was our friend, and the thought of some wacko just murdering him like that—for nothing—it makes both of us crazy."

"I understand," Drew said.

Julie began to compose herself, and Drew asked detailed questions about exactly where they entered the property, how they got to the location where they found the bones, how often they went over there and what Brian's favorite spots were. The women answered all of his questions, with he and Mike taking notes. Tommy left the note-taking totally to Mike, partly because Mike was the junior man of the team, but also because Tommy was renowned for having a mind like a steel trap. He had been known to recount almost verbatim information that his part-ner kept in notes—without ever reading the notes.

Drew indicated he was finished with his questions, and nodded to Mike and Tommy. Tommy looked thoughtful, and then cleared his throat.

"What other spots did Brian frequent in his bird watching? He didn't restrict that activity just to the old Gunther place, did he?"

"No," Frances answered. "He liked to go down by the livestock tank on Mr. Parker's place, and along the creek that ran through his place and then on into the old Erickson place."

"But you didn't search any of those places, right?"

"No, we didn't," Julie said. "We knew he didn't go to either of those places. We knew he had gone to Gunther's that weekend."

"How did you know that?"

"The bird he was looking for was there, and Mr. Gunther had given him permission to go to that part of his place anytime. You know, it's three hundred acres out there, Detective. We didn't have to traipse across the whole three hundred," Julie said.

Tommy smiled and nodded. "You knew where to look for the evidence."

"We knew where to look for the *bird*," Julie said defiantly. "And we knew about Brian's alternate exit."

Tommy smiled broadly now. Julie knew what he was trying to do, and she was prepared to stand her ground. In that moment I saw a different Julie than I had seen before. I saw the strength of her love for Brian.

"Good," Tommy said. "That's all I needed to know."

When they were through questioning the women, we went back out to the farm and talked to Mr. Burkhardt. He was ten years younger than my dad, but he was decrepit. He wheezed and shuffled and was all bent over. I couldn't imagine how this old man ever got on a horse. It was probably all his crankiness that aged him so much. His wife was there, too, and she seemed very pleasant in contrast to her husband.

Drew questioned Burkhardt about going out to that part of his farm, and whether or not he ever noticed anything strange going on out there. Burkhardt cussed and carried on, and basically told Drew he never went out there, never saw anything suspicious and he didn't appreciate trespassers being on his place. He was completely cross and uncooperative, and Drew Smith was fed up. Burkhardt had already effectively stonewalled this case. If it hadn't been for the gumption of Julie and Frances, we would have been nowhere. Then Burkhardt told Drew how lucky Julie and Frances were that he hadn't shot either one of them.

"Well, Mr. Burkhardt, you're actually the lucky one there," Drew replied.

"What in blazes are you talking about?" Burkhardt grumbled.

"Posting a No Trespassing sign isn't a license to commit homicide in the State of Texas, sir. You might be able to report someone for being on your property, and have them arrested. You could also prosecute them for being there, but you cannot shoot them unless they are inside your home. If I ever have to come out here for a dead body on account of your shotgun, I will be hauling your sorry, cranky behind into the hoosegow on homicide charges. I would personally make sure you never see the outside of Huntsville State Penitentiary again. Do I make myself abundantly clear?"

"Hmmph," Burkhardt grumbled.

Drew stood to his full six-foot-four-inch frame, and repeated, "I asked you if you understood me, sir."

Mrs. Burkhardt moved to the edge of her seat with a scowl on her face and spoke. "The lieutenant asked you a question, Carl."

"I heard him." He looked up at Drew. "I heard you, and I understand," he said grudgingly.

"Good. 'Cause I get riled when I have to come clean up behind homicides—particularly for nothing more than a conflict over a man-made boundary."

Drew had completed the interview of Mr. Burkhardt and you could have heard a pin drop in that room. With that we left the Burkhardts' home and headed back to Austin. I don't think Drew and I spoke more than ten words the whole way back.

✧ Chapter Sixteen ✧

The victim from Hempstead was a man in his early thirties. That meant that Addie's death was the anomaly as far as gender was concerned, but everything else seemed to fit otherwise. We had been fooled as to the identity of the remains that turned out to be those of Brian Ferguson. I didn't want to make false assumptions again.

The man had been shot in the head, as Addie had been; however, he had been shot three times—once directly in the face. It made my work difficult, but not impossible. The crime lab had done a good job of putting all the bones back together.

The reconstruction was well under way when Drew came by with the packet of photos I had asked him for. I offered him some coffee or tea, but he declined saying he had to get back to work. He did want to see the reconstruct, so I took him into the studio.

The bust of the Hempstead victim stood on the table near the middle of the room. I had all the tissue-depth markers on it, giving it an ominous appearance. One of my big swing-arm work lamps was on and shed light across the whole area. Drew stood in front of it and nodded.

"So, how long before this thing develops a face?"

"Patience, Lieutenant Smith. You cannot rush this work. I'm going pedal-to-the-metal as it is."

"All right, so when?"

"Give me another couple of days and I'll be done."

Drew sighed, but knew he'd have to wait. I wasn't going to work all night on this just to finish it. I had done three reconstructs in an unbelievably short time frame already. I needed to take more time with this one.

Drew left and I went into the kitchen and made myself a cup of hibiscus tea. While I waited for it to cool a bit, I took the photos out of the envelope and began to lay them across the table. The site was as chilling in the photos as it had been in person. The horror of what had been done there—the murders of at least three people, their burial here and then their exhumation. It was unthinkable and puzzling, and I wanted answers.

I called Leo Driskill. She had heard about the Hempstead find from Tommy. I told her I had crime scene photos and she said she definitely wanted to come over and look at them. She was about to go on duty, so she would come over as soon as she could to see what I had, but it wouldn't be today.

I sipped my tea and went back to work on the bust. Two hours later, I had laid a good bit of clay between the tissue-depth markers and finished my tea. I stood up and stretched and looked out the back window of my studio. It was midday and time for lunch. The face on this one was shaping up, and the more I worked, the more I wanted to know the answer.

The bust on the Hempstead victim was done now. I had done what I said I wouldn't do. I had worked all day and through the night to finish it after my visit with Drew the day before. Just wanting to know had fueled me to pull an all-nighter. The face was staring back at me now. An oval, narrow face with a square chin, a slender nose and a high brow line. I had taken a Polaroid of it, scanned it and e-mailed it to Drew.

He had called me five minutes later and said he was on his way over with news. I looked awful. I hadn't slept and I was wearing my work clothes. I had clay in my hair and it stuck out all over the place. Again, the short haircut was my saving grace.

I pulled the dried clay out of it, got up off the stool, then went into the bathroom and ran water through my hair and combed it. I looked pretty good for a mature chick who'd had no sleep and no shower.

I went into the kitchen and made more tea. I was standing there listening for the doorbell, when the phone rang. It scared the daylights out of me. I picked up and it was Chris.

"You sound like something warmed over more than a few times," she said.

"Thanks. And I look so lovely, too."

"Well, this will perk you up."

"Lay it on me."

"The guys at A&M called, and all the soil samples match. That means both of the samples from here and the ones the State Crime Lab just took from the Hempstead site. They all have the same composition—mineral for mineral and microbe for microbe."

"That's what I expected. The news just keeps getting better."

"Definitely."

I was about to tell her I had finished the bust, when the doorbell rang. I signed off with Chris, promising to call her and give her the latest update after I talked with Drew.

Drew was in "uniform," so to speak, and as I would have expected. He was wearing the trousers, white shirt, his Texas Ranger tie, boots, badge, gun and western hat so familiar to Texans as the symbol of their elite in law enforcement. He took off the hat as he entered the house and we made our way into the kitchen.

"I smell hot tea," he said, smiling.

"It's green tea with jasmine. I made it just for you," I said.

"Liar," he said jokingly.

"Okay, so I made it for you and me."

As I poured two cups, Drew sat down and placed an envelope on the table, then laid his right hand on top of it.

"Don't keep me in suspense, Drew Smith. I've worked too hard for you in the last two days for you to be jerking my chain."

He chuckled. "All right, all right."

He opened the envelope, slipped a piece of paper out and slid it across the table.

"It's the Texas driver's-license photo of a man by the name of Doug Hughes," he said.

I looked at the photo and my heart felt as if it skipped two beats. It was the same face as the one on the bust I had just made.

"Another dead-on image, Dr. Antoinette. As usual, you just keep making it easy for me." He smiled broadly now.

Leo came over the next morning to see the crime scene photos from Hempstead, as promised. We went into the kitchen and I made tea for both of us.

"Well, I have news that I haven't shared with you yet," I said.

"Give."

"I finished the bust yesterday, and took a Polaroid and faxed it to Drew."

"And?"

"It's Doug Hughes."

"Good work, Toni."

I handed her the crime scene photos that Drew had given me, and then I went back to finish our tea while Leo pored over the photos. She asked question after question and I briefed her on every detail I could think of. Then she put her tea mug down and went silent. I sat at the table and sipped my tea while I watched the wheels in her head turn. Then she spoke.

"I have more of a theory now."

"Okay."

"This larger site is probably where the other two were buried and I suspect this third one was buried there with them. I think the killer dug them up and moved the other two for some specific reason. Brian because of his mother. Addie because he wanted to be rid of her, but wanted the water to carry her off. He dug them all up and moved Addie and Brian. What's significant here is that he took the bones from Doug and just dumped them back in a grave and covered them up."

"Why do you think he did that with Doug but not Addie, too?"

"I think it was partly guilt over killing her, maybe wanting to get rid of the remains so he could 'forget' about what he'd done, but maybe also to get her away from *him*." She pointed down at one of the photos of the skeleton.

"Jealousy after death?"

"Sure. Why not? The killer was messed up enough to kill them in the first place. This isn't a rational thinker here. In his, or *her*, mind revenge is still the motive for all of this. He may feel guilt over the death of Brian, and maybe a twinge of some guilt about Addie, but his revenge would be overpowering when it came to Doug. Doug would be the primary focus of his blame and his revenge."

"Jimmy claims that Addie and Doug were not involved, Lori isn't commenting much to any of us, and Dody says for sure they were involved."

"None of that really means anything," Leo said. "Jimmy could be lying, Lori is unbalanced and Dody is a drunk. So who knows? Besides, remember what I told you about a killer like this not having to have real evidence of what he believes. What he believes could be in his mind."

"Or not."

"Or not. It could be real, and this is all the result of incredible rage. It happens all the time."

"So he kills both of them, but he shoots Doug three times."

"I think the fact that Doug was shot three times is meaningful," Leo went on. "But I think the fact that he was shot twice in the head, once in the face, is even more significant. There was real contempt in this killing, and in the haphazard reburial. He didn't want us to find Doug, but he thought the remoteness of the burial site itself would prevent that. So, even though he didn't want Doug found, he also didn't want to spend any time or effort on the reburial. So he just provides a shallow grave and dumps the bones in. He's still angry about what Doug did."

"Well, if it weren't for our trespassing bird-watchers we never would have found this place. In fact, animals probably would have eventually carried off the bones."

"Probably, and I imagine he knew that."

"Thanks to Julie and Frances he was wrong."

"They were friends of Brian's?"

"Yes, and they literally risked their lives going onto that property nosing around. They knew we couldn't get a warrant, but those ladies were determined to have answers about Brian's death."

"Incredible."

"Yes, it is."

"I believe that Brian had no connection with Addie and Doug. When I look at the way each of them was killed, and how the reburials were handled... I believe that Brian was in the wrong place at the wrong time. I think he was a witness, and he was killed to ensure his silence."

"Yes, I agree."

"I think that's why it became so important to the killer to move Brian so he could be found."

"He was the only innocent one."

"Exactly. We're going to have to connect the killer with one of the crime scenes somehow, you know."

"Well, Jimmy Hughes lives here in Austin, where the remains of Addie and Brian were reburied."

"That's not going to be enough."

"So, what is the connection to old man Gunther. Who is this Mr. Gunther anyway?" Leo asked. "Do we know anything about him? Maybe he has some part in all of this. The body was found on his farm."

"Mr. Gunther is dead. The old guy who lives there now isn't Gunther, he's not even related to Gunther. He just bought the property from the family when Mr. Gunther died. They just call it by that family's name because of how long they owned it."

Leo nodded. "Okay, but you said y'all had trouble with the owner of this place."

"Yeah, his name is Burkhardt—Carl Burkhardt."

"So, then maybe Burkhardt has something to do with all of this."

."It doesn't fit, Leo. He didn't own the place until five years ago. The bodies were originally buried there sixteen years ago."

"I'm trying to find some connection between this burial site and the victims—other than our birdwatcher. We already know his connection to the site. What in blazes were Addie and Doug doing there?" Leo got up and paced. "How is the crime lab doing with the evidence they found at this site?"

"We'll get all the results in the next couple of days."

Leo nodded and sat back down at the table, focused on the photos again. About that time, the phone rang, and it was Drew.

"Toni, you are not going to believe what the crime lab came up with."

"What?"

"An old medallion. It was wrapped around some of the bones of Doug's hand."

"What kind of medallion?"

"It's a heart, and has something engraved on the back."

"Spill it, Drew."

"It says, 'For Lori.'"

"So it belonged to her and it was found with him?"

"Right. Also, Lori is missing, Toni."

"Get out."

"I'm serious. We went to pick her up for questioning and the woman is gone."

"Did anyone check with Jimmy Hughes?"

"Way ahead of you. We went over there, and she was not there. He claims he has no idea where she is, and he's not talking. I don't have probable cause to bring him in, and he's not going to tell us where she is, if he knows."

"I'm going over to talk to him."

"Toni..."

"No, Drew. I'm going. Leo's with me. I'll take her, and you can't stop me."

He sighed. "All right, Toni, but call me and fill me in right away."

"You got it."

I explained to Leo what was going on, and we piled into the Mustang and took off for Jimmy Hughes's house. When we got there, he was in the living room playing his guitar. He was hesitant to let us in, but I begged him to let me in and let me talk to him. He let us both in.

"I don't know why all you people keep thinking my business is any of your business."

"Listen to me, Jimmy. Your brother's remains were found in Hempstead."

"I know that. That Texas Ranger told me that yesterday."

"Jimmy, they've found a medallion that belonged to Lori. It was in the grave with Doug. It looks bad for Lori. The Texas Rangers are looking for her, and they will find her. It would be better if you just told us where she is."

Leo spoke up. "You know, Jimmy, she could probably claim some kind of diminished capacity in her defense."

He squinted and looked at both of us intently. "Defense!"

He stomped around the room and turned to face us again.

"Y'all don't know anything. You want to get into everybody's business even though it has nothing to do with Doug's murder. Lori didn't kill anybody. I didn't kill anybody. That medal y'all are talking about is one that Lori got from her grandma, and she gave it to Doug. He wore it all the time—never took it off."

"Jimmy, I saw Lori down at Mrs. Ferguson's house in Houston. How do you explain that?"

He sat down in the chair and put his head in his hands. Leo and I sat on the sofa across from him and waited. He began to cry softly. He looked up at us with tears in his eyes.

"I loved my brother, and I already told you there was no way he was having an affair with Addie. Now I'll tell you how I know. It's none of your business, but I'll tell you 'cause I want you to leave her alone."

I looked over at Leo, and we both waited. Jimmy rubbed his hand over his face and looked down again. I could tell he was trying to keep his composure, and I did not know what to expect.

"Lori left and moved to Georgetown after Doug disappeared, because since Doug disappeared, he could not marry her, and that was a problem, because she was pregnant. Folks in Viola and Rock Hill don't understand things like that. They would have persecuted her. Lori was distraught—because Doug was gone, and because she was pregnant. And everybody was saying he was having an affair with Addie Waldrep—bunch of gossips and liars."

He choked and put his head in his hands again. We waited for what seemed like minutes but it wasn't.

Jimmy looked up, and his chin quivered. "My little brother was a sweet guy. He would never do that to Lori and then mess around with Addie. He loved Lori. He was going to marry her. He was a great guy, not stupid like me."

He stood up now and walked over and faced the wall.

"When he disappeared, Lori came to me for help because she was afraid to tell anyone else. I've been helping her out ever since."

"Jimmy, where is the child?"

He turned around and looked at us both.

"I helped her. I took care of her. I wanted her to move down here so I could help her out more, but she didn't want to live in the city, so she stayed up in Georgetown. So I went up to help her as much as I could, and I took her to the hospital when she went into labor."

He walked over to the chair and sat down again. He was becoming more emotional. He was leaning over, looking at the floor.

"My nephew was born dead." He was sobbing now and put his head in his hands. "She named him James Douglas Hughes, and I came up with the money, and we buried him in a little cemetery in Georgetown. Lori has never been right since. She's been in and out of the hospital for her problems. I look after her 'cause she's family to me."

"Oh no," I said.

I felt horrible. This was why he was evasive. This man was trying to protect the honor of a woman his brother had loved.

"Now maybe y'all see why I wouldn't say. All these bodies start showing up—first Addie, then that Brian guy. Lori started having more problems again. She thought she was going to talk to that Ferguson lady and ask her if she knew where Doug was. Can you believe that?"

He shook his head. Tears filled his eyes and flowed over his scarred face.

"She saw you there at Mrs. Ferguson's, and she got scared and left. She came to me to tell me about it. I got her calmed down, and I thought I got her kinda back on track. Then that Ranger told me they found Doug—" he wept harder now "—I had to tell her. I can't lie to her."

"Of course not, Jimmy."

He shook his head. "She ain't missing. I had to put her back in the hospital. The news about Doug broke her. In her mind she's been thinking all this time he would come back. She won't even talk now. I don't think she'll ever be right again."

He put his head back down in his hands and just sobbed harder.

Leo and I sat there, not really knowing what to do, and then I gutted up and went to him, and kneeled next to him and put my arms around him.

"You did the right thing, all the way down the line, Jimmy. None of it is your fault. You did all anyone could do, and more. I am so, so sorry for everything."

He put his head on my shoulder and sobbed for a good five minutes.

Leo and I sat in the Mustang for a couple of minutes without talking. We were stunned, and I for one was ashamed of myself. I knew there was no way I could have known, but I was ashamed anyway—but I was proud of Jimmy Hughes—proud and amazed at his integrity. Jimmy Hughes gave chivalry a whole new definition.

Leo finally spoke. "Well, I guess we both know that he's no killer."

"That poor girl."

"And Jimmy, too. Their lives have been totally wrecked by all this."

I was supremely frustrated. Frustrated over the predicament of Jimmy and Lori, and frustrated that we had no evidence to tie a killer to this crime.

"That whittles down our suspect list," I said.

"It has to be Dody, or else it's just some psycho who randomly killed them all. That last scenario doesn't fit what the crime scenes say, but Dody as killer does."

"Okay, so how do we tie him to any or all of these crime scenes? He lives outside of Austin, and I don't know of any connection he has to Hempstead, and no one there recognized Addie. If Doug and Addie weren't involved with each other, how and why were they in Hempstead. Did Dody follow them there, or take them there?"

Leo nodded. Then I thought about everything Leo had said previously about the burial site, about a connection between Gunther or Burkhardt and the killings, about what Addie and Doug would have been doing in Hempstead, and then I thought about something Dad had said.

"Hey, kid, want to go get the best pie you ever had?"

"Huh?"

"Let's take a little ride up to Viola and see my new friend, Doris."

Leo agreed reluctantly. I think she only agreed because she knew I must have a reason. We were dazed after the visit to Jimmy, and we had nothing else to go on. I cranked up the Fastback and we took off.

On the way up, I gave Leo the lowdown on Doris. I wheeled the Mustang off of the state highway and onto the farm-to-market road that led to Viola. Leo and I arrived at the Main Street Café in less than an hour. It was lunchtime and the place was full of all the locals. Leo and I had decided on the way up that we would do the whole lunch thing. Doris greeted us at the door.

"Toni!" she exclaimed. "Hon, it is so good to see you again. Who's your little friend here?"

"Doris, this is Lieutenant Leonie Driskill from the Austin Fire Department."

"You're a fireman, hon?"

"Yes and no. I was a firefighter in active combat, but now I'm a fire investigator."

"An investigator—well, now, that sounds real interesting. So, do y'all work together sometimes?"

"Yes, we do," Leo replied.

"Y'all want a booth?"

"Yes, Doris, that would be nice," I said.

"Good, because I have one right over here that would be perfect for you two ladies. Now y'all look at those menus and I'll be right back to take your orders."

We made our decisions and took our time enjoying our lunches while Doris took care of her lunch crowd and got them all fed and cleared out. I think the whole town must have been there that day. Doris definitely had a full house. When she was finally done with all that, Leo and I had finished our meals.

"Y'all want pie?" she asked, winking at me.

"You know I do," I said. "And you know what kind."

"Alrighty, apple for you with no ice cream. What about you, hon?" She looked at Leo.

"What's my other choice besides apple?"

"The other choice is my homemade chocolate-cream pie. It's icebox pie, hon. Know what I mean?"

"Yep. Load me up with chocolate cream," Leo said.

"Don't tell her to load you up until you've seen the size of the normal pieces," I advised.

"Okay then, don't load me up, but bring me your normal slice."

Doris chuckled as she walked off. She returned in short order with two plates, and slid the pieces of pie in front of Leo and me. I thought Leo's eyes would pop out of her head when she saw the size of that slice.

"Wow!" she exclaimed.

"Save your 'wow' until you've tasted it," I told her. "You're going to exhaust your superlatives too soon."

She put a forkful of that pie in her mouth and within a millisecond the blue eyes began to roll.

"Oh man!"

"Told you," I said with a mouthful of apple.

Doris was delighted, of course. She lived for those moments of extreme praise.

"You ladies make me feel good. I'll go and get you some coffee to wash it down with."

Doris made her way to the coffeepot and brought back two cups and set them down for us.

"Doris, can you sit with us for just a bit? I have some questions to ask again."

"Hon, I was wondering when you were going to get around to that. I would love to sit down for a bit. I've been on my feet since six this morning."

Doris sat next to Leo. I told her about Brian and his friends from Hempstead. I told her all about Doug being found in Hempstead on some farmland and that it looked like the original burial site.

"I just want to go over this again and make sure that you can't think of any connection that might have existed between Addie and Hempstead, because I never asked you that question."

"No, hon, you did not," Doris said. "And you didn't tell me that boy Brian was from Hempstead, you said Houston—and it said Houston on the news."

My heart skipped a beat. I was hoping for all I was worth that I was onto something.

"His mother lives in Houston and that's where he grew up," I said, "but he moved to Hempstead and lived there at the time of his disappearance."

"Well, Addie don't have no connection to Hempstead, hon, but Dody sure did."

Leo nearly choked on her pie. My eyes were wide as saucers.

"Well, go on, Doris."

"Well, Dody's family is originally from there. His granddaddy lived there. Of course, his mama and daddy are both dead, so they don't have no ties there anymore, but back in the day they sure did."

"Did Dody or Addie ever live there?" I asked.

"Oh no, hon. Dody's granddaddy lived there and then he died. I think Dody had an aunt and uncle who lived there for a while, but I think they're gone now, too."

"Whereabouts did Dody's family live in Hempstead?" I asked.

"Near Angler's Point."

My heart came up into my throat I was so excited. I almost held my breath.

"What was their name, Doris. Do you know?"

"Well, of course I know, hon." She looked at me suspiciously. "Why does that matter?"

"Doris!"

"Well, all right, then. It was Gunther. Does that mean anything?"

I exhaled and put my head into my hands, and then ran my hands all the way through my hair and looked up at Leo.

"Oh man," Leo exclaimed. "You have done it!"

"Done what? She's done what?" Doris asked.

"I found the one missing link we needed, Doris— the one missing link."

"How did you know? How did you think of it?" Leo asked.

"It was something Daddy said about how the killer wouldn't have picked that site by throwing darts on a map. There had to be a reason they were there. You said something one time on another case about killers being in their comfort zone. And earlier today you were confused by the burial place where Doug was found being called the old Gunther place when Gunther doesn't live there anymore. You were trying to link it to Burkhardt. The names were different."

"Yeah, so?"

"So, I thought about how the names were different, and about how that was confusing. Then I thought of another reason names are sometimes confusing, and I thought about me and Daddy and how my name is Sullivan and his is Kennedy..."

Doris said, "The Gunthers are Dody's mama's kin!"

"Right." I nodded.

"They're his maternal relatives, so the names are different," Leo said, shaking her head.

"Right. So we never made the connection to the name of the place and to Dody."

"I'll be! You mean to tell me that evil little man buried her and Doug and that other boy up there on his granddaddy's place?" Doris exclaimed.

"Yep. Only it isn't his granddaddy's place anymore. It belongs to a cranky old coot named Burkhardt."

"That wicked little man killed them and that boy Brian?" Doris asked. "Why did he kill that poor Brian boy? Oh my!" she said, slapping her hand over her mouth in realization.

"Now, Doris, you have to keep this under your hat. You cannot tell anyone. I'll tell you all the details later, if you keep it all a secret. We have no proof at this point, and we don't want him to get away."

"Well, I certainly do *not* want him to get away. So, how do you go about getting proof?" she asked.

"Well, we may have it soon. The Texas State Crime Lab is working on it, and what you have just told us helps a lot."

"It does?"

"Yes, it does. Do me a favor, Doris, and don't talk to anyone about this right now. I'll let you know sometime in the next few days when you can tell, but for right now, I need your help and I need you to keep it all confidential."

Doris grinned and then popped her chewing gum real loud.

"Like one of those informers for police that you see on TV on them crime shows." She nodded her head and widened her eyes.

"Exactly," I said.

Doris clapped her pudgy hands together with her long red nails making a clicking sound.

"This is exciting," she said. "I'm happy to do whatever you ask, Toni."

I reached across the table and patted her on the arm.

"You've been a tremendous help through all this, Doris. I'll make sure that the Texas Ranger we're working with knows what a great resource you've been."

"Texas Ranger," she said in a hushed voice.

"Yes."

"Ohhh, when y'all are done with the case, bring him for pie. A Texas Ranger right here in my café. Wouldn't that be the limit? The people in this town would all know I helped solve the case, and the Texas Ranger came to say thank-you and eat pie." She grinned from ear to ear.

I only hoped I could talk Drew into it.

Chapter Seventeen

It seemed that death had been following me lately like a little, ugly black shadow. Never before in my career had I done so many reconstructs at once. I was tired—not physically, but emotionally. I felt I had almost no time to decompress and regroup in between each one and it was wearing on me mightily. I needed a vacation on an island somewhere, but not Hawaii this time. I was thinking Patmos in the Med—some reflection and meditation there and time on the beach to sit and watch the boats go by. A month without bones or reconstructions or murder cases.

I had called Drew on the way back from Viola, and had left him a message to call me. I was sitting at home on the sofa decompressing with a cup of hot chamomile tea, when the doorbell rang. It was Drew. He came in and I got him some tea, and we sat down on the sofa together.

"So, how did it go?" he asked.

I filled him in on all the details about Jimmy and Lori. He shook his head and looked sad. Then I told him about my brainstorm.

"Leo came over today and looked at the crime scene photos and she and I were brainstorming and she got confused over the reference to the old Gunther place and thought the crank who lived there was Gunther. So I explained it to her."

"So?"

"So, then after we found out Jimmy and Lori weren't suspects in all this, I started thinking about the confusion over the names, how that family hadn't lived there in a while, etcetera."

"And?"

"I drove Leo up to Viola and we had pie at the Main Street Café and talked to my friend Doris."

"Now who's jerking whose chain, Toni?"

I grinned. "Dody's mother's family had a place down at Angler's Point near Hempstead. It was his granddaddy's place. His granddaddy's name was Gunther."

"No way!"

"Yep. So, with that bit of evidence, don't you think we have enough to connect Dody to the crime scene and maybe make a case?"

"We have more of a case than you think, my friend. While you were tracking down that all-important piece of information, I was doing a little legwork myself."

"I'm waiting..."

"You know Dody has had a lot of jobs in the last fourteen years."

"Yes," I said impatiently.

"Two months ago Dody had a different job than the one he has now."

"Drew!"

He laughed. "All right, Toni. He was one of the crew on the sanitary sewer job."

"Sanitary sewer job?"

"Yes, you know the one the city of Austin had going down at Red Bud Isle two months ago."

"Oh man! Drew, that is sweet!"

He laughed and clapped his hands together. "And that's not all, Toni."

"There's more?"

"Mmmm, hmm," he said, sipping his tea. "The lab got hair and fiber samples out of the crime scene in Hempstead. Stuff that they say is fresh. They sifted that soil and found evidence in the grave itself."

"How do they do that?"

"I don't know. It's what they do. They sift that stuff and bag everything. It blows my mind. They look at it under microscopes, put it into centrifuges and gas chronometers. It's incredible."

"So, you think they'll match fiber or hair samples?"

"I hope so, but that's not all. Our murderer left a wadded-up hankie there."

"Where?"

"In the hole, under the dirt. Apparently, he used it and just threw it down or lost it. It got covered up with the bones. You know, he never thought we'd find them, and if it weren't for those women and their 'bird-watching' outing, we never would have."

"A hankie?"

"Yep. Now, the fiber I don't hold out much hope for. It seems like too much of a needle in a haystack to me, but those forensic people never cease to amaze me, so who knows? We do have a hair sample and fluid in the hankie. We can match the hair under a microscope and we can match both with DNA."

I shook my head.

"You know, Drew, he was probably six sheets to the wind when he dug them up. He's drunk all the time from what I can tell. I imagine he saw Mrs. Ferguson on television and got all upset about her son, and went off down there in a drunken stupor, did all of his digging and reburying, dropped that hankie and never realized it."

Drew nodded. "Yeah, and that property would be easy to get on to. For all that Burkhardt's bravado, he's so bent over, he couldn't possibly police all that land."

"After your lecture the other day, I don't imagine he'll be policing much of anything."

Drew grinned.

"So, what's next?" I asked.

"I'm outta here is what's next. I was on my way to get a court order for hair and DNA samples from Dody Waldrep, and now I am totally fired up to do exactly that."

"Great, but before you go, I just want to know one thing."

"All right."

"Do you like pie?"

Chapter Eighteen

Drew and I got out of the car, and Tommy and Mike got out of their car behind us. The State Crime Lab had made an exact match on the hair sample from Dody Waldrep. They were still working on the fibers, and the DNA would take a while, but the hair, combined with what we knew about Dody's connection to the burial site, was enough for an arrest.

As we began to approach the house, Dody came outside onto the front porch with a shotgun in his hand. He had a wild look in his eye.

"Stop where you are," he screamed, but we had already stopped.

Dody's thin wrists trembled and his weathered fingers wrapped the gun barrel like a rope binding.

The weapon was pointed somewhere between Drew and me and I was afraid Dody would discharge it inadvertently with his tremors.

"Dody, don't you think you've killed enough innocent people already?" Drew asked calmly.

"Innocent?" he screamed. "They weren't innocent! Adulterers! Fornicators!"

"Not Brian, Dody. He wasn't an adulterer. He *was* innocent."

"The young man," Dody almost wailed. "I didn't mean to kill him. Tell his mama I didn't mean to..." His voice trailed off and he began to sob softly.

"His mama on the television begging for someone to come forward about him—that's what did it, isn't it, Dody?" Drew said. "That's why you dug them all up."

Dody began to sob more. "I had to take him somewhere someone would find him. I had to—for his mama. I didn't mean to kill him."

"Why did you dump Addie by the river, Dody?"

"I didn't want her to be with him. I didn't want them to be alone together."

"So, you reburied Brian somewhere he could be found?"

Dody nodded, but was sobbing heavily now. Sweat was pouring down his face and running into his eyes and mixing with his tears. I was growing more nervous by the second about that shotgun.

"What about the others? You didn't want any-one to find Doug Hughes, but you wanted her found?"

Dody shook his head, and through his sobs he said, "I didn't think anyone would ever find her. I thought the river would get her. I didn't want to leave her out in the open, but I thought the water would come up and take her."

"The women who found Doug, they weren't part of your plan either, were they, Dody?"

"They weren't supposed to be on private prop-erty! What were they doing there anyway? Snoop-ing around—trespassers, that's what they were! I wanted his bones to rot in the ground till the end of time!" He had become more agitated again and he began to shake more now.

There was moisture all over my face and neck. It was humid there in the warm afternoon air sur-rounded by all those trees and with no breeze. I looked over at Drew. The man was as dry as a bone. His arms hung loosely by his sides and his hands were open and relaxed. I expected to see his right hand near his service weapon. In my pe-ripheral vision I saw my son begin a slow move to-ward the weapon inside his jacket. Drew's arm came up slightly with his palm toward Mike, indi-cating that he should stop. It was a slow, con-trolled move. Drew was all about self-control. Mike lowered his hand.

"Dody, it's all done now. The only way you can make things right with yourself and God is to confess what you've done. It's your only hope."

Drew Smith was making a sincere plea. He believed what he was saying. He wanted to close the case, but he was also concerned that Dody would condemn himself beyond all hope—the kind of loss of hope that lasts beyond this side of life. He always saw in his work both sides of the tragedy. In Drew's mind there were always at least two victims in a homicide—the murdered and the murderer. I understood this view and shared it. I saw the deviation of the murderer as an evil that had taken root and then spread to include other innocents as well. Drew once told me he always thought of how each killer had been an innocent child once and somehow it had all gone wrong. It was a fact that disturbed him, but also drove him in the way he did his work.

Dody trembled all over and shook his head vehemently. "No," he sobbed. "No, I ain't confessin' nothin'. I did what I had to do."

Drew's calm voice continued, "Dody, no matter what your wife and Doug Hughes did to you, they did not deserve to die. And the young man, Dody, you shot Brian Ferguson to cover up your deeds. He didn't do anything except appear at the wrong place at the wrong time. That wasn't 'what you had to do.'"

Dody was sobbing so hard now that the barrel of the gun lowered just slightly.

Great, I thought. If it goes off, he'll just get my kneecaps now.

"You took the young man from his mama, Dody. Her only child and you took him. His daddy's dead and now his mother has cancer. She's buried her child next to his daddy and soon she'll join them both. You took everything they had. You have to come clean, Dody—no excuses. No excuses." Drew was calm, steadfast, his voice almost sympathetic in its litany of guilt.

Dody's sobbing became hysterical now and he dropped to his knees. The shotgun clattered onto the porch in front of him. He put his hands up over his face and all I could see was the heaving of his chest. Then the wail of his grief and guilt came forth. Birds fluttered frantically from the surrounding trees at the sound of the calamity. Drew was calmly walking up to the porch. He claimed the shotgun as Dody continued to cry aloud. Drew laid the gun off to one side and gently took one of Dody's arms and cuffed it. As Dody continued crying, Drew carefully helped him to his feet, and as he did so, he clasped Dody's other arm, cuffing both arms behind him.

In a gentle but firm voice, Drew began, "Dody Waldrep, you're under arrest for the murders of Adelaide Waldrep, Doug Hughes and Brian Ferguson. You have the right to remain silent. Can you hear me, Dody?"

Dody nodded, his sobbing becoming quieter now.

"You have the right to have an attorney present during questioning..."

Drew continued with the Miranda rights, questioning Dody after each one to make sure that he was listening in his state of mind.

Once Dody was properly Mirandized, Drew led him to the squad car and assisted him into the back seat. Tommy retrieved the gun from the porch and he and Mike got into their car.

Drew climbed behind the wheel of the car and Dody said, "Sheriff?"

Drew looked into the rearview mirror at Dody. "I'm a Texas Ranger, Dody. My name is Lieutenant Drew Smith."

"Oh," Dody said with a slightly confused look on his face. There was a brief silence and then he said, "Lieutenant, will you tell the boy's mama that it was an accident that I shot her son?" Dody looked totally beaten. He sniffled and continued. "Tell her I shot him before I even knew what I done. Tell her I got sick and threw up and I been sick ever since. Will you tell her I didn't mean to and I'm sorry?"

His declaration was heartfelt, but even still Dody would not admit the fullness of what he had done. He wanted to believe, and to have everyone else believe, that killing Brian was something other than a murder to cover murder.

Drew looked into the rearview mirror at Dody as he spoke. He paused a moment and I could see he was considering what to say. Then he sighed and said, "Yes, Dody, I'll tell her."

Drew started the car. Then I noticed something I had never seen before—the slightest bit of moisture just inside the lower lid of Drew's eyes. He turned the car around and we headed back toward Austin in silence.

Dody was booked into the Travis County Jail pending trial, and within two months he was dead from heart failure. His daughters had buried their mother's remains in the local cemetery at Viola, but they refused to claim their father's remains, so he was buried in the county cemetery under a cheap marker. I will always believe that it was the poison of over sixteen years of guilt, and his failure to fully accept that guilt, that killed Dody Waldrep, but even Chris didn't have the power and authority to list "Guilty Conscience" as a cause of death.

❧ *Chapter Nineteen* ❧

A few weeks after Dody's arrest, Sergeant Major Tomlinson called me from CILHI to tell me that CILHI had accepted my findings and had officially declared the remains as those of Theodore P. Nikolaides. I asked him that before they made the official call to Irini they allow me twenty-four hours to tell her myself. The sergeant major agreed that would be acceptable.

I had given her the news weeks before when I had told her the results of my work. Now I could call her and tell her it was official. I made the call. She took it well. The initial shock and pain of the confirmed reality had worn off and adjustment was settling in. The agony of over thirty years was beginning to be assuaged. Total closure would come soon—for all of us.

* * *

Irini had told her children and they were flying to Washington, D.C., for the funeral. Arrangements had been made to ship the casket there to Andrews Air Force Base. It would be transported with a military escort to the church in D.C. Reverend Iordani had been requested to officiate at the service and he had obtained the appropriate permission.

When the body, such that it was, arrived at the church, Irini and Reverend Iordani and I were there to meet it. Irini's children, Eleni and Gregory, were due in that evening, along with my son, Mike. Meanwhile, prayers of blessing were to be said.

As Reverend Iordani began the prayers, Irini wept softly. When he was finished, Irini turned to me.

"I cannot see the bones."

"You don't have to," I said.

"Okay. Because, I cannot see them. I cannot look at bones when what I have in my heart and my soul is the face and the smile of Teddy."

"I understand," I said.

It was actually a relief. I had worried about how she would react when she saw what was left of him.

I was staying at a hotel near the Washington Mall. I decided to leave the hotel early to give myself time to go by the Vietnam Veterans Memorial Wall before going to the church for the funeral. I told Mike I would meet him at the church.

When I arrived at the Wall, I started on the low end and walked slowly behind a small group of people who were there to see the great landmark. The panels were arranged by date of death and each name had a diamond next to it, unless the person was an MIA. If they were an MIA, there was a plus sign next to the name. This had no religious significance, as the symbol was only used because it was an easy shape to turn into a diamond if the MIA's remains were recovered and identified, or to turn into a circle if the MIA was discovered alive. Unfortunately, there were no names on the Wall with circles next to them.

I finally arrived at the panel that contained Teddy's name. I ran my hand down the list until my fingers found the name Theodore P. Nikolaides. There was the dreaded diamond next to his name. For years now, I had periodically made trips here to look up the names of people I had known during the war and always there was one name without the diamond. In my mind, the symbol next to Ted's name had not been a plus sign, but a cross. A sign of hope for me—hope for life, hope that maybe it could become a circle, even though I knew better. Somehow, Ted's death seemed less real then. Now I couldn't even absorb it—not even with the diamond staring back at me, not even after having my hands on his skull and sculpting his face back to life in the clay. I left the Wall and made my way toward the church, hoping to find the truth in my faith, as I had so many times before.

Michael and I walked behind the family at Arlington National Cemetery, with the black, flag-draped gun carriage ahead of us. The military personnel, somber but crisp in their dress uniforms, escorted their fallen comrade, showing their respect with snap turns and rigid, deliberate salutes. I looked out across the sea of white grave markers—a sea of fallen heroes and statesmen. Too many dead—too many still missing.

When we reached the burial site, they lifted the casket off the gun carriage and placed it on the supports over the grave. In the cool wind of that early-spring morning, the American flag waved in the breeze with the air force flag. Not far from them, the black flag of the POWs and MIAs also fluttered.

The air force pallbearers and the gun detail stood at attention on one side of the casket until the command was given for them to stand at ease. They all stood that way while Reverend Iordani once again chanted our beautiful hymns of faith and life and hope.

Reverend Iordani held in his hand a beautiful cross, which he had bought for Irini in remembrance of Teddy. When he got to Irini, he handed it to her and spoke words of comfort to her, gave a blessing to her family and then uttered the words "Ζωη σασ," which mean "Life to you all."

The command came for attention and the gun detail fired a salute of three shots. As the final shot echoed through that hallowed ground, taps began to play and two of the pallbearers began to fold the flag that rested across Teddy's casket.

With the flag neatly and tightly folded into a triangle, the senior officer approached Irini, made his precision snap turns, bent down and handed her the flag with the words "Please accept this with the thanks of a grateful nation."

We all stood as we heard the echoed breathy rumble of jets approaching for the flyover to pay homage to their fellow pilot. Irini stood with the flag in one hand and the cross held tightly in her other, tears streaming down her face. Irini's son, Gregory, stood on one side of her and her daughter, Eleni, stood with her husband and young daughter on the other side.

I stood at the graveside looking over at Greg, who looked so much like the father he never knew. I watched Teddy's oldest child, Eleni, weeping into the shoulder of her husband, Pete Spiropoulos.

Their five-year-old daughter looked up at Pete and whispered, "Daddy, Pappou's sleeping now."

Pete nodded, squeezed her small hand and held his wife tighter. Eleni looked at the casket of the father she barely remembered, but had loved and mourned all these years. In that casket his remains finally lay at rest. I never told her or her brother and mother how little of him there was. All they knew was that the skull was in good enough shape for me to do a reconstruct. I couldn't bear for them to know that my friend Teddy, who at five-ten stood so much larger than life, had been reduced to a skull and a handful of bone pieces no bigger than large pebbles—the sacred rubble of an unholy war.

As the jets flew over in missing-man formation, and the one plane separated and flew away from the others, I thought how like Ted's soul it was—free at last from the prison of his anonymous grave. Not only that, but I thought how like Ted himself that plane seemed—the way he had lived his whole life—independent and strong, soaring above the rest. At last I bowed my head, thanked God again for his life and wept the tears of over thirty years.

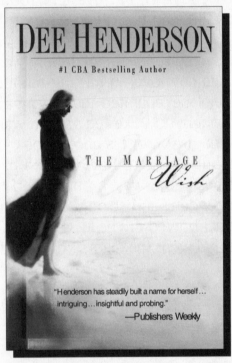

GOLD IN THE FIRE

BY

MARGARET DALEY

A string of burning barns worried firefighter Joshua Markham—his quiet town, Sweetwater, was at the mercy of a serial arsonist. Yet it was a beautiful woman trying to save her family's horses that took his breath away. Darcy O'Brien and her young son needed a chance to start over, but neither Joshua nor Darcy was ready for a relationship, as their respective pasts had left them wary. But when the arsonist struck close to home, would Joshua risk everything for the woman he loved?

Don't miss

GOLD IN THE FIRE

On sale October 2004

Available at your favorite retail outlet.

A NEW LIFE

BY

DANA CORBIT

Her matchmaking friends thought single mom Tricia Williams
needed someone, and the blind dates began. No one could
compare with her lost love—until she met Brett Lancaster,
the handsome new man in town. But their budding
relationship grew strained when Tricia learned he was a
state trooper. She'd already lost one man to a risky job. She
didn't know if she could put her trust in God once again
and find the strength to begin a new life…with Brett.

Don't miss

A NEW LIFE

On sale October 2004

Available at your favorite retail outlet.

A town scorned them both.
Could faith and love bring them together?

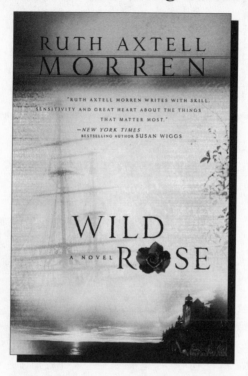

All her life, Geneva Patterson had known what it was to be an outcast. Plain, awkward, thought to be unmarriageable, she endured the cruel taunts of townspeople in solitude. But then she encountered a man who made her dream that there could be something more for her....

Caleb Philips, too, was an outcast. Once a respected sea captain, he'd been accused of a shameful crime. Geneva believed in Caleb's innocence. She longed to help this proud, unyielding man find redemption in the town's view—and in his own—through God's grace and a woman's love....

On sale October 2004.
Visit your local bookseller.

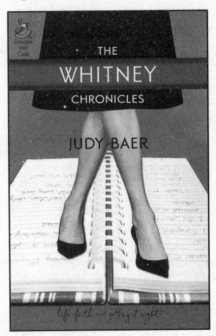